A Duke By Any Other Name

The Brides of North Barrows #2

CLAIRE DELACROIX

Books by Claire Delacroix

For information about Deborah Cooke contemporary
romances and paranormal romances, please visit:

HTTP://DEBORAHCOOKE.COM

PROLOGUE

Airdfinnan Castle, Scotland—December 1811

Alexander Magnus Armstrong, Duke of Inverfyre, read his aunt's letter again and frowned. It was after dinner and he was alone in his library, the darkness of the night pressing against the windows and a robust fire blazing on the grate. He had been looking forward to an entire winter of savoring the pleasures of home.

The letter meant his desire was not to be.

He poured himself a port in consolation, took his favorite seat by the fire and sipped as he read the letter again. The last thing Alexander wanted to do was to abandon his sanctuary and ride for Cornwall, but it appeared that he had little choice.

He had baited a trap and his prey was poised to

1

seize the cheese. It would be irresponsible to surrender the chase now.

Even if his sister Anthea would be disappointed.

Alexander frowned. His aunt, a baroness who had worked her way into every ballroom in London, was also his primary source of information. Penelope sent him chatty letters at regular intervals, cleverly managing to include all of the intelligence he needed amidst the drivel of who had cut whom and who had pawned their silver, substituting sterling for plate. No other soul could have read this missive and noticed the one gem of valuable information amidst the gossip.

In the employ of the crown, Alexander hunted criminals who preyed upon high society. He had been in pursuit of a jewel thief for a year. He had guessed long ago that the villain was the same man who had seen Anthea blamed for his crimes during her first season, but soon Alexander might be able to prove it. He had to catch the scoundrel in the act. A gentleman and gem collector who had experienced losses due to this very thief was aiding in the hunt. Mr. Timothy Cushing had shown the Eye of India to many in London and was dispatching it to the perfect recipient.

Alexander's aunt shared the news that her good friend, Mr. Cushing, would be giving the fabulous brooch as a surprise to Lady Tamsyn Hambly, who was being married at Castle Keyvnor in Cornwall at Christmas. Aunt Penelope speculated on the bride's delight at this surprise, for truly, who would not be thrilled?

Clearly, Alexander would also be spending Christmas in Cornwall, although not at Castle Keyvnor. The local village and its tavern would have to do.

He considered the calendar. Since it was only the beginning of December, he could arrive in time by carriage if he set out immediately.

He grimaced, for he was not yet ready to don his foppish disguise again.

Findlay entered with a tray and inhaled sharply, probably because his master had already poured his own port and was simultaneously making a face. "I apologize for the delay, Your Grace," he said quickly. "Or is it the quality of the port that causes disfavor?"

"Neither, Findlay. You were neither late nor remiss. I was bored with my aunt's tattle and too impatient to wait. Any blame is entirely mine."

The older man stole a glance at Alexander as he wiped the decanter and ensured that all was as it should be. "Is there any detail that I can repair, Your Grace?"

"No, Findlay. You will never change my aunt." Alexander smiled, then folded the letter and tucked it into his pocket. He surveyed the cozy library and sighed. "I will be departing at first light with the coach and six. I'll want the black team again, though Rodney will not be pleased to have them run again so soon."

"If he knows now, Your Grace, he will ensure

that they are pampered tonight."

"Yes. The big coach, please. It gives me more room to stretch my legs."

"Oh, Alexander!" Anthea said from the doorway. "You can't be leaving. You've only just returned home." She looked to be on the verge of tears and Alexander hastily finished his port. At a telling glance, Findlay filled his glass again.

It was well established at Airdfinnan that the Duke of Inverfyre could not bear the sight of his sister's tears.

"I fear I must, Anthea, but will return as quickly as possible." Alexander nodded to Findlay. "Perhaps you could see to the details."

"Of course, Your Grace."

Alexander could see that Findlay was itching to know where he was going and why, but the older man didn't ask. "Could you send Haskell to me to discuss the packing of my portmanteau, as well, please?"

"Your portmanteau, sir?"

"Yes, I will be gone for at least a month, probably longer."

"Alexander!" Anthea protested. "What about Christmas?"

"You will enjoy the festivities without me." When she might have protested, he lifted a hand. "I am somewhat irked to be leaving again so quickly, but there is nothing to be done about it. Dr. MacEwan insists that I take the sea air in Cornwall in December."

To Alexander's dismay, a tear not only slid down Anthea's cheek but she came into the library to sit opposite him and make her appeal. "Dr. MacEwan," she muttered under her breath and dashed at her tears with her fingertips. "Is the air in January truly so different in Cornwall?"

"So he insists."

"I think him a fool. You are more hale than any seven men I know."

Findlay bowed and departed, so obviously wanting to linger and eavesdrop that Alexander smiled.

The change in his expression evidently encouraged his sister to speak her mind. "Of course, you would not have to worry so much about your health if you had an heir," she reminded him yet again. "High time it is, Alexander, for you to take a bride."

"Anthea!"

"It is fearsome quiet at Airdfinnan, Alexander, especially at Christmas. It would be much merrier with little ones underfoot." She smiled. "I wouldn't miss you so much if there were half a dozen children here."

"Then you should accept a suitor and have children of your own," Alexander suggested gently.

His sister blushed and dropped her gaze, her expression like a dagger to his heart. "Not I," she said softly, then forced a smile. "And it is you who must have a son to ensure the succession, after all. Is there a woman behind this speedy departure, or a

5

damsel in distress?"

As much as he liked the bright gleam of curiosity in her eyes, Alexander could not lie to Anthea. "There is no damsel, in distress or otherwise."

Anthea made a face, then stole his glass, taking a tiny sip of the port. "I do not believe your health is compromised. I suspect you simply want away from here."

Alexander laughed. "Away from Airdfinnan is the last thing I desire." He could not keep himself from casting a longing glance over the library and its comforts.

"Then you should wed. You'd have every excuse to remain home then and it could only improve your health."

"Perhaps I will wed after you do," he teased.

"Perhaps I should wed after *you*," Anthea countered. "In fact, I will make you a wager, Alexander."

"Ladies do not wager, Anthea. Surely Mama taught you that."

"Surely she did, but I would like to, all the same." Anthea had her stubborn look, which was all too rare these days. It seemed she seldom cared sufficiently about any matter to be stubborn, and just the sight was enough to make Alexander take her wager, whatever it might be. "You always wish for me to return to London and society, at least for a season. I will go with you and your bride, once you choose to wed."

"Anthea!"

Anthea sat back, looking pleased with herself. "So, the sooner you wed, brother, the sooner I will follow go to London and find a husband."

"You mean to make a wager you will not be required to fulfill," he jested. "For each of us are as set against marriage as the other."

To his surprise, Anthea shook her head. "No, that is not true, Alexander. I would love to marry and to have children." Her tone was so wistful that he was prepared to find her a spouse this very night. "But it must be the right man, for I would have the same kind of love as Mama and Papa shared."

"Theirs was a rare bond."

"So, I must dream of what is mundane, instead of what is rare and precious?" she replied, her tone light. "Alexander, are you the brother I believe I know so well?"

He laughed. "A man has more time to linger over such a choice than a woman."

"Indeed, and I am already twenty-five, Alexander. You had best hurry to find your lady wife."

"It is not so simple as that..."

"No, it is not," Anthea agreed, interrupting him. She leaned forward, her skirts rustling as she removed something from her pocket. "Mama warned me of that. She told me to find a partner who was honest, and one with no secrets, one whose nature I could admire and whose appearance gave me pleasure. She told me the rest would follow."

"Did she?"

"And for you, I would add that your bride should be young, so she will have had less time to have cultivated secrets. You will be the one to teach her of many worldly matters, and she will adore you for it."

Alexander was amused. "Is that how a good marriage is contrived?"

"It will be so for you, I am certain of it. Here, I have a token for you."

Alexander extended his hand. Anthea dropped something small and round into it. It was black and about the size of a pea. He held the small dark sphere to the light, suspecting that he knew what it was. "A seed?"

Anthea laughed. "Not a seed, Alexander, *the* seed. The seed from the vine of Airdfinnan, from the last time it grew and flowered."

"That is a fairy tale!" Alexander had heard the fanciful stories about the thorned vine that covered the walls of his castle and home, that it was from a seed brought back from the crusades by a knight, that after its arrival at Airdfinnan it grew only when the laird of Airdfinnan met his bride-to-be. He certainly did not believe that its perfume abetted the laird's courtship and conquest.

But Anthea clearly did. "It is not! Mama told me that it grew when Papa courted her, and that she had never seen the like of it. She told me that its perfume was like an enchantment. Papa's mother advised her upon your birth to save the seeds for your courtship."

"Mama gave me several herself, before she died. They never grew, Anthea, which is proof that the tale is nonsense."

"It is proof only that you had not met the lady who could claim your heart. Certainly, Miranda Delaney, no matter how fine her lineage and how lovely her countenance, would never have held your affections for long. What a viper!" Anthea's disdain was clear, though the very mention of Miranda's name reminded Alexander what a fool he had been. "Her memory should not be of sufficient merit to keep you from happiness. That is why the seed did not grow."

Alexander tossed the seed into the air and caught it. "And what would you have me do? Plant a seed each time I meet a pretty woman?"

"I would have you seek a suitable woman, one who is honest and true, and pretty enough to tempt you, just as Mama advised."

"And young."

"And young," Anthea agreed. "And if she is amenable to your attentions, I would have you plant the seed, so that the vine might aid your suit."

Alexander drained his glass and set it aside, rising to his feet with purpose. "I suppose this errand cannot wait?"

Anthea laughed. "I should not delay in your place, Alexander, not if I wished my only sister off the shelf next season."

"You are relying upon my taking this wager."

Anthea took a deep breath. "I am seeking inspiration, Alexander. I know I should wed. I know I should leave Airdfinnan." He watched her pleat her dress with nervous fingers. She swallowed and he ached at the sight of her unhappiness. "I know I should return to London and put all the rumors to rest." Her gaze met his. "But I am afraid, Alexander."

He dropped to his knee before her. "You know I would go with you, and defend you..."

She silenced him with a touch. "I know, but it would be so much easier to go with you and your wife, if she is your beloved. Your happiness would give me strength, and she would be able to accompany me where you cannot go."

She was so lovely in her appeal that Alexander felt her will becoming his own. He had always been damnably susceptible to feminine beauty, and the malady had become more acute while he hunted the thief. The fire caught the red-gold of Anthea's curls as if to toy with it, and her blue eyes were wide. She looked fragile and vulnerable and he wanted nothing more than to see her hand placed in that of a deserving and honorable man. Even her conviction in the truth of the tale of the vine was compelling to him on this night.

He bent and touched his lips to her fingers. "I will try, Anthea."

She smiled. "That is all a person of sense can expect, Alexander."

Alexander had no sooner put the seed into the

pocket of his waistcoat than his valet tapped once upon the door, then entered the library.

Rupert Haskell was of an age with Alexander, the youngest son of a baron who had lost his father's favor. He had chosen to earn his way and Alexander had been glad to give the other man a position. Haskell had a keen affection for travel and a similar loyalty to the crown. He had dark hair and a ready smile, but his wits were quick and his blade was quicker. He was a good man to have at one's back, particularly in Alexander's chosen profession. He was completely in Alexander's confidence and when alone, they spoke as friends, not as master and servant, for they had been such at school.

Haskell spared a quick glance at Anthea, as if surprised to find her there, and color rose on the back of his neck.

"I will leave you to your arrangements, Alexander," Anthea said, rising to her feet. "Godspeed to you, for I'm certain you'll be gone before I rise in the morning." She kissed Alexander's cheeks then left, barely sparing Rupert a glance.

Rupert looked after her with an unmistakable yearning in his gaze, at least until Alexander cleared his throat. The other man then closed the door. "Where?" he asked, mouthing the word more than saying it aloud.

"Cornwall," Alexander said, replying in kind.

Rupert crossed the room and noted the letter on Alexander's desk. He smiled. "Your aunt?"

"Just as planned."

"The full rig?" Rupert asked, referring to Alexander's disguise.

Alexander sighed and nodded, then sat at his desk to respond to his aunt.

"Thank goodness those salmon and lemon striped trousers were delivered before we left London," Rupert said more loudly. "You'll be quite the sight, Your Grace."

Alexander gave Rupert a poisonous glance, knowing that his valet enjoyed his flamboyant clothing a little too much. "There will be stealthy work to be done, as well," he said in an undertone. "Bring the black, and my favorite boots, too."

"You could just stay home, or leave it to another."

Alexander impaled him with a look for the very suggestion. "My chase. My kill."

"I know." Rupert smiled then bowed. He raised his voice. "I shall see the portmanteau packed immediately, Your Grace, and be prepared to leave at dawn."

"Excellent, Haskell."

The other man left the library, admitting a cool draft that made Alexander think of cold carriages, draughty taverns and stone castles in Cornwall cold enough to freeze a man's marrow. If he had a wife, he'd have warmth in his bed, to be sure.

But if he had a wife, he'd have a wealth of other problems.

Like having a wife. It was one thing to be less

than completely honest with Anthea, but he doubted he could hide the truth of his profession from a wife.

And that meant he would have to completely trust the woman he married. Given his experience with feminine deception, Alexander thought that unlikely to occur soon.

Still, Anthea's proposed wager was her first sign of interest in marriage in years. He removed the seed and rolled it between his finger and thumb, considering.

It could not hurt to try again. He didn't imagine for a moment that the old stories were true, but Anthea would expect him to make a report upon his return. Perhaps if he tried, even if the seed failed, that would be sufficient to coax her back to London for the season.

It was more than worth a try.

That prospect put a smile on his lips. He lifted his quill and dipped it into the ink, thinking of how best to use their established code.

My dear Aunt Penelope—

What a delight to arrive home and find your letter already awaiting me here. It appears the post does not dally as I do! And such news! You make me yearn again for London. I regret that I will not be back in Town soon, for my doctor, the excellent Dr. MacEwan, has insisted that I take the sea air in Cornwall this month. He recommends ten thousand deep breaths a day—ten thousand!—and I heartily doubt that will leave me sufficient time to pen you a single line...

CHAPTER ONE

I wish we could go faster," Daphne complained, looking out the carriage window yet again. "Why are the horses so slow? We should have reached the next tavern by now!"

Her younger sister, Eurydice, who was so oblivious to the marvels of the fashionable world that Daphne sometimes doubted they were truly siblings, looked up from her book. "Getting to Castle Keyvnor sooner won't get us to London sooner. May is *months* away."

"But we'll be in London for the new year," Daphne replied, impatient to begin the adventure of her coming-out season. Her sister didn't know that Daphne had made a wish on Stir-Up Sunday, a wish that by Christmas a year from now, she would be married to a rich duke. The further they rode from North Barrows, the greater the likelihood of there being a duke in the vicinity.

London would be thick with them.

"I can happily delay the expense of our upcoming venture," her grandmother said with some acidity. Octavia Goodenham, the dowager Viscountess of North Barrows, raised a hand when Daphne's alarm must have shown. "You'll have your season, my dear, then Eurydice will have hers as well. A promise made is a promise kept."

Nelson, their grandmother's maid, nodded and smiled primly at the supreme good sense of her employer. Jenny, the maid for the girls, watched and listened as always she did. The five women were packed into the carriage, for the weather was a foul mix of rain and wet snow, and *Grandmaman* refused to let Nelson or Jenny ride outside. Daphne sat beside her grandmother on the bench that faced forward, while Eurydice was opposite her. Nelson had the window opposite Daphne's grandmother, and Jenny was wedged between Eurydice and Nelson. The young maid was sniffling and shivered at intervals, which was why she'd been given the warmer place in the middle.

"I would rather go to the Continent and save you the expense of a season, *Grandmaman*," Eurydice said. "For there are fine museums there, and I would prefer to visit them than find a husband."

"A husband will do you more good in the end than a glimpse of a statue," their grandmother retorted. "If he is chosen well."

"I will have a duke, *Grandmaman*," Daphne said. To wed well, preferably to a wealthy duke, had been her ambition since the death of their parents. She ignored how Eurydice snorted. Her sister thought it was a vain and silly goal, but Daphne had sound reasons for her scheme. Eurydice didn't remember very much of events after they had news of their parents' death, but Daphne still had nightmares about those days of uncertainty. "You need not fear for *my* future."

Nor would she have to worry about Eurydice's future. Daphne would take care of her sister forever.

"You might be right," the dowager replied. "You are pretty enough to tempt a man's eye, that is for certain."

"If Daphne becomes that rich, then I won't have to marry at all," Eurydice said, as if she had guessed Daphne's secret scheme. "I could become a governess, like Sophia." She referred to Sophia Brisbane who had left their service after winning the affections of Lucien de Roye at Castle Keyvnor just months before.

Their grandmother straightened and fixed Eurydice with a glare. "You. Will. Do. No. Such. Thing."

"But, surely it matters what *I* desire..."

Daphne looked out the window to hide her smile, for she knew that Eurydice could not win this argument, at least not while *Grandmaman* drew breath. After that, if Daphne succeeded, her very clever sister would be able to make her own choices, however unconventional they might be.

She had to wed a duke.

A rich duke.

Surely her wish on the Christmas pudding could only help?

"Surely not!" *Grandmaman* said to Eurydice. "You will desire what you are told to desire, which can only be an affluent husband. After that, you may appeal to him to decide what you are permitted to desire. The matter will be out of my hands."

Eurydice looked as if she might argue that, but Daphne kicked her, hiding the move beneath her skirts. She couldn't bear if they argued all the way to Cornwall. Eurydice's lips tightened but she fell silent.

Grandmaman shook her head. "Though all this racing about may end my days." She appealed to Nelson. "We only just returned to North Barrows and caught our breath, and now it's back to Castle Keyvnor again."

"Indeed, my lady," agreed the maid.

Jenny nodded, though she had not been with them on the last journey.

"And not to celebrate Christmas at home." *Grandmaman* sighed. "It does test one's patience."

"But it might be quite lovely and festive, my lady," Nelson dared to suggest.

"A Christmas wedding is *so* romantic, never mind a double wedding," Daphne agreed. "What do you think the brides will wear?"

"Does it matter?" Eurydice asked.

"Of course, it matters! When I marry my duke, I will wear a dress the color of champagne," Daphne said. She closed her eyes, perfectly able to see herself in the dress in question. It greatly resembled one she had seen amongst the fashion plates at her grandmother's dressmaker, a confection of silk and lace that had haunted her imagination ever since.

"You'll be all yellow then with your blonde hair," Eurydice said. "I will wear red when I marry."

"You will not!" *Grandmaman* declared. "If it's not the rushing about that finishes me, it will be the pair of you!"

"You will survive us all, *Grandmaman*," Daphne said soothingly.

Her grandmother harrumphed and rapped her umbrella on the floor of the carriage. "I will see you both married at the very least, though it may be the last deed I do."

"Let us not hope for that, my lady," Nelson said with vigor. "I'm certain you would like to see each of the girls deliver their first son."

"You are right, of course, Nelson." *Grandmaman* nodded with resolve. "Clearly, I shall have to live a good deal longer." Her eyes flashed. "But I will faint with hunger if we don't reach the next tavern soon." She tapped her umbrella on the roof and roared with a vigor that indicated her demise could not be imminent. "Thompson! Why do we proceed so slowly?"

Daphne wondered whether the driver would pretend that he hadn't heard her grandmother. He would have to have been deaf to have missed that shout. She wiped the condensation from the inside of the window and peered out into the rain. The carriage leaned as they took a corner, and she caught a glimpse of the road ahead.

She gasped, then polished the window a little more to get a better look. "There's a coach and four ahead of us, with an insignia on the door." All of the occupants of the carriage straightened a little at the prospect of a diversion. Even Eurydice looked up from her book. Unfortunately, the road had straightened and they had completed the turn, so one glimpse was all Daphne would have.

"Who is it?" Eurydice asked.

"I don't know, but there are six black horses pulling the carriage!"

"Six. And the coach?" *Grandmaman* demanded.

"Very large. Black, as well, with gold trim. It seemed to have flourishes of gold upon the doors."

Her grandmother inhaled. "How many footmen?"

"Two on the back, *Grandmaman*, plus the driver and one other."

The dowager nodded and narrowed her eyes as she peered through the glass. "I know that coach. There cannot be another so fine as far north as this."

"Whose is it?" Daphne demanded.

"It was made in France for the Duke of Inverfyre when I was a young bride."

There was a duke in close proximity?

Daphne was delighted.

Her grandmother continued. "I remember the old duke bringing it home. Oh, he made certain every soul saw it between Portsmouth and Airdfinnan, including your grandfather and me." She nodded. "It was quite marvelous. I wonder how well it has been maintained."

Daphne sat back in defeat. A duke her grandmother considered to be old must be ancient indeed. Eurydice grinned, for she had undoubtedly guessed her sister's dashed hopes, and Daphne longed to jab her. She had to ask. "The duke is old, then?"

"Old?" her grandmother echoed. "He's dead. His grandson inherited the title, for the old duke's son died before him."

"How long has the new duke been married?" Eurydice asked.

"He isn't," *Grandmaman* admitted and Daphne smiled, her hopes restored. "He's quite eligible, at least on paper, but he's not married."

On paper?

"I don't understand," Daphne said when no one else spoke.

Grandmaman smiled and patted Daphne on the knee. "It means, my dear, that I don't recall his name being linked romantically with that of any woman."

Daphne sensed that her grandmother meant more than she was saying, but she couldn't imagine what it might be. "Then he hasn't found true love yet?"

Grandmaman laughed. "If he has, it won't be with a woman."

This made no sense to Daphne at all.

To her relief, Eurydice seemed to be similarly mystified, so for once, she wasn't the last one to figure something out.

"And a great shame it is, to be sure. The family are most affluent. There is a decided aversion to gambling in the Armstrong line, matched with a good fortune with investments that is almost unholy." *Grandmaman* twirled her cane. "It is said that this duke's fortune is one of the greatest in all of England. Pity about his preferences. If his sister does not marry, that great lineage might come to an end."

Preferences? Daphne and Eurydice exchanged a glance of confusion.

The carriage slowed and turned, and they heard Thompson whistle.

"Ah, here we are," *Grandmaman* declared with a decisive tap of her umbrella. "And not a moment too soon, for I am ravenous." The door was opened and one of the footmen put down the stool for the dowager viscountess. Another held an umbrella high so she wouldn't have to use her own for the short walk to the tavern. "Ah!" she declared as she alighted. "You will soon see what I mean, my dears. The duke is also taking refreshment here. I shall remind him of our family's acquaintance."

Daphne squeezed Eurydice's fingers with

delight, then emerged from the carriage herself, her heart thundering.

She should have made a wish sooner.

She stared in shock at the man speaking to her grandmother near the doorway to the tavern. He smiled and bowed over Lady North Barrow's hand, his manners impeccable and his clothing so garish that Daphne didn't know what to say or do.

Eurydice gave her a hard nudge from behind. "Move, you goose," she muttered. "We can't get out because of you and it's freezing cold."

Daphne took a few steps, still startled to silence.

A moment later, Eurydice halted beside her. "Oh!" she said, apparently similarly astonished.

Grandmaman raised a hand to beckon to them, and the duke turned to survey them with polite curiosity. His waistcoat was a splendid and hideous garment, made of a vivid blue cloth thick with gold embroidery. Eurydice said something through her teeth, but Daphne ignored her. The duke raised his quizzing glance and peered at them, blinking as if he had trouble with his vision. There was no difficulty with his appetite, for he had a considerable paunch. His cheeks were fat, but his legs were surprisingly trim.

And he was a duke.

"Oh," Daphne agreed, then tried to be gracious. "I don't believe I've ever seen that shade of apricot used with such enthusiasm in a man's garments before."

"It's orange," said Eurydice.

"No, I'm certain he calls it *abricot*."

"You don't have to say it French!"

"I think I do," Daphne mused.

"And with green." Eurydice grimaced.

"*Chartreuse*," Daphne corrected, for she saw definite possibilities in her near future.

"The blue is a horrifying addition."

"*Azure*," Daphne said, then smiled at the duke. He took a closer look. She was glad to be wearing a new dress in the shade of pink that flattered her coloring so well.

"He's wearing more rouge than *Grandmaman*," Eurydice whispered wickedly, but Daphne ignored her. Her sister surveyed her and her eyes widened in horror. "You wouldn't."

"He's a duke," Daphne said mildly, then met her sister's gaze. "Me first."

Eurydice laughed. "You needn't fear any competition from me in pursuit of that silly fop. Look at him! He's a joke from head to toe!"

Daphne smiled. There were no other unwed aristocrats in the vicinity, nor were there likely to be any. She had no competition at all and might very well save her grandmother the expense of a season in London.

For a duke.

Daphne couldn't have cared less how he dressed. His finery was expensive, which meant her grandmother was right about his finances.

He did have fine legs and he was tall.

This was her chance. She crossed the yard with

her chin high and her skirts gathered in one hand.
Her steps were quick and delicate, as if she joined a
dance, and in a way, she did. A thrill of anticipation
coursed through her as she wondered just how
well—and how quickly—she could charm him. Oh,
there was no deceit in Daphne. She meant to make
whatever duke she won a most delightful and
attentive wife.

The duke lifted his glass a little higher to watch
her approach.

Daphne wasn't so innocent that she didn't notice
the glimmer of interest in his very blue eyes as she
curtseyed before him.

What a beauty!

Alexander savored the sight of Lady North
Barrow's granddaughter as she came tripping
toward him, her lifted skirt hem granting him a
glance of her neat ankles, and her cheeks a little
flushed. Her hair was like spun gold and her eyes
shone with what appeared to be good nature. Her
dark green cloak parted as she walked, giving him a
glimpse of her figure. She was slim through the
waist and hips but curved sufficiently to invite a
man's caress. That deep green of her cloak made her
eyes appear to be a deeper hue than they were. The
pink of her dress became her very well and she put
him in mind of apple blossoms in the spring.
Though she was fair, her lashes and brows were
dark, and her lips were both sweetly full and ruddy.

Alexander was certain that he hadn't seen such a splendid beauty in years.

When she smiled at him, he was reminded of exactly how long he had been celibate.

And he completely forgot why.

Indeed, he found himself recalling Anthea's challenge and almost fingered the small seed in his pocket.

Lady North Barrows made curt introductions, as was her way. He hadn't seen her since Anthea's season, but she hadn't changed much. Miss Goodenham's lashes fluttered as she curtseyed before him. He caught a glimpse of creamy cleavage, then she met his gaze and blushed prettily.

Alexander's heart gave a leap, though he fussed over her hand, bending to kiss it with flair. He caught a whiff of her scent then, roses mingled with the perfume of her own skin, and that sent an unwelcome stab of desire through him.

There was a second girl, Miss Eurydice, who was younger, stockier, slightly darker in coloring and who eyed him with suspicion. Lady North Barrows then ushered her granddaughters into the tavern ahead of her, as if they were wayward chicks. Alexander watched them go, telling himself he should be pleased that the dowager viscountess was not intent upon flinging her eligible granddaughters at him, like every other ambitious mama in the *ton*, but in truth he was disappointed to have enjoyed their company for so short an interval.

Even though it was undoubtedly for the best.

To his surprise, Miss Goodenham turned to glance back at him, her remarkable eyes filled with appeal. "But *Grandmaman*," she whispered, loudly enough for him to overhear. "Surely we cannot let His Grace eat luncheon alone. It would be unforgivable."

Lady North Barrows paused in the midst of giving instruction for their meal to her maid, which she wished to have served in a private room. She eyed him, her misgivings more than clear. "We would not wish to intrude on His Grace's meal," she said, her tone chiding, and Miss Goodenham appeared to be so disappointed that Alexander almost spoke out.

Instead, he took out his snuffbox and fussed over a pinch, ensuring that he looked a perfect fool. The working men regarded him with disdain, but that was part of the plan. His disguise kept anyone from looking closer.

No sooner had Alexander savored his snuff and stepped into the tavern, then Rupert appeared and bowed. "Your Grace, all has been made ready for your luncheon."

"Thank you, Haskell. Is there a fire? I cannot bear the cold in this place! And is the soup very hot?" He shuddered elaborately, then ran a finger across the top of a table. He eyed his glove with distaste. "I hope it is *clean*, Haskell."

"Of course, Your Grace." Rupert bowed once more and smiled. "I have ensured that all will meet with your approval."

"And dessert?" Alexander whined. "I must have a choice of *two* desserts."

"There is only one pudding, Your Grace, but I will fetch some oranges from the carriage."

Alexander sighed. "I suppose that will suffice. One must endure so many hardships while travelling." He waved to the ladies with his lace-trimmed handkerchief and followed Haskell, ensuring that his steps were mincing. He then held that handkerchief to his nose, as if the smell of the tavern was too much for him to endure, and heartily regretted losing sight of Miss Goodenham.

He couldn't help but overhear the discussion Lady North Barrows had with the proprietor.

"I apologize, my lady, but there is only one private chamber," that man informed her with a bow. Alexander paused to listen. "We seldom have such noble guests. If you would like to take your meal in the far corner, there, I will have that fire set..."

"In the *tavern*?" the dowager protested. "It is unthinkable! Surely you have some chamber available."

"I am sorry, my lady, but..."

Alexander cleared his throat. "How large is the chamber where I shall dine?" he asked Rupert.

His man bit back a smile. "It is a fair size, Your Grace. I am certain you will have every comfort there."

"Is it of sufficient size that the ladies might join us?"

Miss Goodenham turned to him, her eyes alight with pleasure and her lips parted. Zounds, but she was an alluring creature!

Was she as conniving as that beauty, Lady Miranda Delaney, had been? Alexander wished very much to know, although already he doubted as much. There was something open about her expression, something that hinted at an honest heart.

He couldn't help but recall his sister's list of attributes in a potential wife. *A suitable woman, one who is honest and true, pretty enough to tempt you—and young.*

Miss Goodenham appeared to have every quality on that list.

The seed seemed heavily in his pocket.

"There is no need, Your Grace," Lady North Barrows began to protest, for undoubtedly she did not wish to be in his debt.

"There is every need when the comfort of three ladies is at stake," Alexander said with a bow. "I insist that you accept my hospitality and dine with me this day. Our conversation will pass the time pleasantly until we continue on our separate ways."

"Oh, *Grandmaman*, what a wonderful invitation!" Miss Goodenham enthused. "Surely we cannot decline such generosity?"

"Surely we cannot," Lady North Barrows said grimly. She gave a stiff curtsey. "I thank you, Your Grace. Your kindness is most welcome."

"The pleasure will be all mine," Alexander

replied, then offered his arm to the elderly viscountess. Lady North Barrows hesitated only a moment before placing her hand upon his elbow. He was keenly aware of Miss Goodenham trailing behind him and could not quell his own sense of triumph.

The room *was* of a goodly size, both comfortable and warm. The fire had been stoked up and the table had been set with hearty fare, both hot and cold. There was wine, because Alexander ordered it, and he fussed over the vintage as well as the cushion on his seat. Of course, the viscountess seated them in order of precedence and he was ridiculously pleased to have Miss Goodenham at his left hand.

He wished with all his heart that he might not have been in disguise.

Perhaps he might encounter her again, after this quest was completed, and appear to her as a reformed man.

Perhaps he would ensure that eventuality.

The meal was served and various pleasantries exchanged. Alexander ensured that he slurped his soup loudly and took great satisfaction in the way Lady North Barrows winced at the sound. The viscountess turned and began a conversation with Eurydice, enquiring after that girl's choice of reading.

Miss Goodenham, however, regarded Alexander with shining eyes, apparently oblivious to his bad manners. Was she stupid? He supposed it was possible, though it would be disappointing.

"Your Grace, would you indulge me by telling me of Airdfinnan?" she asked.

"Faith! Why? What would you know about it?"

"What does it look like? Where is it? I have only been to Scotland once, and that was to visit Edinburgh. I did love that city and always wished to see more."

"Airdfinnan is in the Highlands," he said. "Filthy weather there. Cold and snow and rain, then heat and sun and rain." He shivered again. "I endeavor to be there as little as possible." In truth, of course, Alexander would have been glad to retreat to Airdfinnan and never leave his estate again.

Miss Goodenham was not daunted. "I love the rain in Scotland, and the lush green of the hills. I think it may be the most beautiful place in all the world."

Alexander spared her a glance, distrusting that they were in such agreement. "Have you seen much of the world?"

She laughed, a delightful sound. "Almost none of it, but what I have seen of Scotland is so pretty that it seems unlikely any place could be finer."

"Filthy weather," he repeated.

"But you must have a fine house to provide shelter from the elements."

Did she mean to assess his wealth? Alexander saw no reason to hide the truth, for Lady North Barrows could tell her all she desired to know and more. "A castle," he confided. "Built on an island in the river Finnan."

"How romantic!"

"Damp," he said flatly, then lied. "I am never warm when I am there."

"Perhaps you need a wife to keep you warm, Your Grace," she said, blushing at her own daring comment. Her eyes danced though, as if she invited him to smile with her, and Alexander was sorely tempted to do just that.

If not to kiss her. Her lips were enticing.

"Daphne!" Lady North Barrows snapped. "Such impertinence is unnecessary."

"I meant only to make a jest. I do apologize, Your Grace, if you thought me rude."

"Of course not," he said and was rewarded by her smile. "You cannot have had your first season yet."

"No, not yet!" Her eyes shone, reminding him of Anthea's long-ago enthusiasm. "We are going from Castle Keyvnor to London to prepare for it." She reached out and fleetingly touched his cuff. "Could you perhaps give me some advice as to the best shops and dressmakers, Your Grace? A man of your sartorial flair must know where the most talented needles are to be found."

Was she flirting with him? It was unthinkable. Eligible women, no matter how ardently their mothers cast them into his path, invariably fled from Alexander in this guise.

"I know little of women's clothing, to be sure,"

he said, laughing loudly so that the food in his mouth was displayed.

"But I love this color," Daphne said, touching his cuff again and letting her fingers stray to the back of his hand. She flicked a glance at her grandmother who had not noticed her gesture and her eyes were filled with beguiling mischief when she met his gaze again. He did like a little audacity in a woman. "What would you call it, Your Grace?"

"*Abricot*, of course," he said, using the French pronunciation.

"*Abricot*," she echoed perfectly. "I think I shall have a dress made in this hue, with the green, too."

"*Chartreuse*," he supplied.

"That is what I thought it should be called!" she confessed with delight. "It reminds me of spring, which is a welcome thought at this dreary time of year." She bit her lip. "I do not think I could carry the *azure* at the same time, though."

"Perhaps a Spencer?"

"That is a wonderful notion!" Daphne cleared her throat. "That is, if you would not be insulted to be my inspiration, Your Grace." She lifted her gaze to his, an invitation in those eyes that fairly stole his breath away.

It had been a long time since a woman had given him such a welcoming look, and none had ever granted him one while he was in disguise.

Alexander swallowed. "Of course not!" he cried, gesturing with his fork. "One must take inspiration where it can be found. I saw a gentleman in Town in these very colors and knew I had to have a suit of similar gaiety."

"In Town! Oh, I envy you such travels, Your Grace."

She would not be dissuaded. Alexander was in peril of being enchanted by this damsel. "It is the food that I love best there," he confided, then patted his padded belly. "I could eat all the day long there, and invariably, I need to have my waistcoats let out after a sojourn in London."

She laughed lightly. "Perhaps I would have to loosen my stays."

Alexander nearly offered to help with that task, but he recalled himself. He giggled in a frivolous fashion. "Oh, I have to loosen mine!" he confided in a girlish voice.

She faltered only briefly, then fixed her attention upon him again. "But you must find some appeal at Airdfinnan. Surely the hunting is excellent there."

"I am told that it is, and I suppose we do eat game there with some frequency." Alexander made a moue of distaste. "But I could never hunt. To kill something? Never! The blood! The horror!" He waved his hands helplessly, then seized upon his fork and gobbled his roast duck and gravy.

"I love to hunt," Miss Goodenham admitted, much to his surprise. "I've only been once, though. My cousin, the viscount, invited us this autumn after he returned to North Barrows with his new wife. I found it thrilling."

'Thrilling' was exactly how Alexander felt about

the hunt.

Indeed, the quest he undertook was a hunt and he savored every moment of it.

His mouth went dry. It was easy to imagine riding to hunt at Airdfinnan with this alluring beauty by his side.

"I suppose the weather was fine," he said.

She laughed and he'd never heard a more wondrous sound. "It was horrible, Your Grace! It rained and rained. We were filthy with muck, but my cousin took a deer. It was so exciting!" Her eyes shone at the memory, and Alexander found himself shifting on his chair.

This was madness. He could not have any matter in common with this beautiful girl. He should not be tempted. He had no time for distraction.

Not until this mission was completed and the villain brought to justice.

Despite Anthea's challenge.

In the back of his mind, Alexander was already considering the merit of opening the London house early, and journeying there from Cornwall himself. If his mission was successful, he would have to return the gem to Cushing and make his report to the crown, after all. What harm would it be to take the delightful Miss Goodenham shopping?

"Perhaps you are a better man than me, Miss Goodenham," he said with a giggle.

She smiled at him. "Perhaps opposites truly do attract, Your Grace."

Oh, she was bold, and he was charmed.

"Dessert!" he cried, putting down his cup so sloppily that he might have been drunk. His wine spilled. Miss Goodenham had taken only the barest sip of her wine. Rupert filled his cup again, then brought him a pudding.

"Is it apple?" Miss Goodenham asked. She watched as he tasted it.

"I suppose it might be. It needs a rum sauce to be edible," Alexander declared, although it was delicious, and Rupert left in pursuit of that very thing.

"May I be so bold as to ask your destination, Your Grace?"

"Cornwall. My doctor believes that the sea air will be restorative, though I will not bore you with a full list of my maladies..."

"Cornwall!" Miss Goodenham said, interrupting him with delight. He nodded warily. "Well, that is where we are going," she confessed. "To Castle Keyvnor. There will be a double wedding there on Christmas Eve. I think it is so romantic!"

They had the same destination.

Praise be that he had remained consistent with his disguise.

And he would see her again. His heart lurched at the prospect.

Miss Goodenham continued. "We were there at All Hallows, and now we return for the weddings. Where in Cornwall are you destined, Your Grace?"

"My man has booked a room in some place called Bowkum..." He waved to the returning

Haskell as if he'd forgotten their destination.

"Bocka Morrow, Your Grace," Haskell supplied. "The inn is called The Mermaid's Kiss. It is most reputable."

Miss Goodenham was clearly pleased. "Bocka Morrow! Why, that is the village near Castle Keyvnor! Will we see you at the castle itself, Your Grace? We attend the weddings of the two daughters of the Earl of Banfield."

"Regrettably, I am not acquainted with the current earl."

"But you must come and walk with me," she insisted, her hand stealing to his cuff again. "I should so like to see you again, Your Grace."

Their gazes met and clung, and Alexander's heart clenched.

"Daphne!" Lady North Barrows barked. "You have scarcely eaten a bite and we must carry on." She inclined her head. "Although the duke has been most gracious in his hospitality, I am certain he desires a little time to himself. Regrettably, we have no leisure for dessert."

The pudding was set before him again, fairly submerged in a rum sauce, and Alexander hoped the ladies did leave him shortly. There was no way he could eat the entire massive serving, but his disguise meant that he would have to do as much if he were witnessed.

"Regrettably," Miss Goodenham echoed under her breath.

"That is a shame," Alexander said, rising to his

feet. He acted as if he were unsteady and gripped the table, wondering if he could tip the entire thing without injuring any of the ladies. It was a sturdy table, unfortunately, for the feat would have made a fine display of his apparent shortcomings. The ladies rose and each came to express their thanks, as well as to say farewell, and he would not have been a man if Miss Goodenham's sweet smile had not sent heat surging through him again.

What would he give for a single kiss?

He bowed and fussed, and they finally left, the beautiful Miss Goodenham last to depart.

Alexander pushed away his dessert with impatience once they were gone, more than ready to have this final victory behind him. He found himself thinking about the allure of watching a lovely girl being introduced to the pleasures of London.

The seed seemed to wriggle in his pocket. He pulled it out and looked at it, halfway thinking it had changed shape.

As if it grew a root.

He would put it in water when they reached The Mermaid's Kiss. Alexander didn't believe in it, but it couldn't hurt.

And when it came to Miss Goodenham, he was inclined to take a chance.

"You are shameless," Eurydice muttered beneath her breath.

Daphne cast her sister a smile. "In the end, you

will call me duchess."

"He's awful!"

"He's sweet."

"He ate with his mouth open!"

"He's unaccustomed to the company of women."

Eurydice gave Daphne a skeptical glance. "I suppose you think you'll be able to charm him into changing his ways."

"I don't care if he changes actually." Daphne paused and looked back at the tavern, hearing the truth in her own words. There was a face in one upper window, watching. She couldn't make out the person's features, but there was an unmistakable area of peach-toned fabric. She waved, a little surprised to realize how little the details mattered. She liked talking to him, and the rest was irrelevant. People changed over their lives after all, becoming thinner or heavier, balder or more grey. It was their essence that mattered most and she liked the duke. "He'll suit me well, just as he is."

Eurydice climbed into the carriage, her disgust clear. "He hates the country."

"He hasn't seen it at its best. The viscount never favored North Barrows until he took a wife."

"He drank too much."

"He did not. I watched. He gave the appearance of being besotted but he drank very little." Daphne bit her lip. "I wonder why he would do that?"

"Perhaps he drinks so seldom that wine affects him more powerfully."

"Perhaps. But then, how would he have known so much about the vintages?"

Eurydice shrugged, having no ready answer for that.

Grandmaman took her place in the carriage then, and began to dictate orders to Nelson about their stop that night. The girls ceased their conversation, Daphne looking out the window and Eurydice returning to her book. Jenny's sniffle was louder and the girl blew her nose with increasing frequency.

Daphne was thinking furiously. The fact was that her impressions of the duke did not fit together. On the one hand, he appeared to be a frivolous fop, concerned only with his own comfort and desires. On the other, she felt a strange thrill when his gaze met hers, and those blue eyes carried an intensity that did not match his words. His belly was large as if he were fat, but his legs were most fine, and his face—when she ignored the rouge—was both masculine and handsome.

It made no sense.

Perhaps she was wrong. Eurydice was the clever one and she thought the duke was precisely as he appeared.

In the end, it mattered little, though. He was interested in her and she did not care why. Daphne was more than delighted that she would have the opportunity to see the Duke of Inverfyre again, and very soon.

CHAPTER TWO

I t's a remarkable piece," Rupert said, his admiration a perfect echo of Alexander's own. "But then, you've seen the original."

"The resemblance is uncanny." Alexander turned the replica in his hand, letting the candlelight catch the facets of the cut stones. They shone brilliantly, and he was impressed by the workmanship. "I've never seen so fine a fraud. I could only tell them apart when I had the genuine Eye of India in one hand and this counterfeit one in the other, and then only with close examination." He didn't tell even Rupert about the small mark on the back of the forgery, made so that they could be reliably distinguished. Cushing was nothing if not diligent.

The two men were in Alexander's rented quarters at the Mermaid's Kiss. The hour was so late that the tavern had quieted below and they kept their voices very soft as they conferred. Alexander had shed his disguise with relief and sat at the table before the fire in his shirt, boots and breeches. Rupert had drawn the drape and locked the door before Alexander removed the pin from its hiding place.

The pin, which was a duplicate of the one being sent to Lady Tamsyn, was oblong in shape and filled Alexander's palm. In its middle was a large cut oval sapphire of deep blue color, as large as the nail of Alexander's thumb. It was surrounded by cut diamonds in glittering ribbons, the whole set in platinum.

At least, the original was a sapphire with diamonds set in platinum. The one Alexander held was glass and paste set in tin. He tilted it toward the light and smiled. "Look. Even the eye portrait has been faithfully reproduced."

"Eye portrait?" Rupert leaned closer.

"It's a piece that was originally exchanged between lovers. That's why it's called the Lover's Eye. The original recipient was given the gem by a lover, and this is a portrait of his eye."

"Who was he?"

"No one knows, but Cushing has contrived a tale that Jonathan Hambly had it made for Emily Hawkins but never gave it to her due to her early and sudden death. That's why he's sending it to the bride, who is the oldest daughter of the current earl."

"Quite a generous gift."

"Remarkably so.

"Won't she be suspicious?"

"Cushing is believed to be eccentric and, in my experience, people are most willing to accept rich gifts, even with meager explanations. Cushing *is* a distant relation." Alexander slipped the gem back into its velvet sack, knotted the drawstring, then placed it into a second velvet bag. Even the bags containing the real gem and the copy were perfect replicas, which made his task much simpler. "You confirmed that it was delivered today?"

"By Cushing's great-nephew, as anticipated. Nathaniel Cushing."

Alexander nodded. "Then the exchange must be made tonight."

"Are you certain you should go alone?" Rupert asked, peeking around the window shade. The evening was clear, the moon nearly full. Alexander might have wished for a few clouds to better hide his activities, but he would make do.

He donned his dark jacket, a large soft hat and his hooded cloak. He tugged on his boots and shoved his gloves into his belt. "Absolutely. You may have to pretend to be me in my absence." Alexander smiled at the very thought.

"Good Lord!" Rupert exclaimed, imitating Alexander's foppish tone very well. "Is there no decent flame to be had in this hovel?" He raised his voice, sounding shrill. "This chimney smokes beyond belief and the bed is as cold as ice. Go and fetch more wood for the fire, Haskell. I don't care what these barbarians have to say of it!"

The men exchanged a glance and a nod, then Alexander unbolted the door. "Aye, Your Grace," he said gruffly, knowing he was not as good a mimic as his friend. "Immediately, Your Grace."

"Well, don't stand there, letting in the draft," Rupert whined. "I already have a sniffle and you know I can't tolerate a chill. Hurry, man!"

Alexander strode from the chamber, but he fetched only one load of wood for the fire. He descended as if to gather a second load, but left the tavern instead. It would take him a good half hour to walk to Castle Keyvnor by a circuitous route, and he could only hope that there were few souls abroad at this hour to notice his passage.

Daphne awakened when Castle Keyvnor was dark and quiet, her heart pounding and her palms slick. It had been her familiar nightmare again, the one in which *Grandmaman* passed and they were left close to penniless.

Again.

Eurydice did not recall that fortnight between the news of their parents' death and *Grandmaman*'s return from Bath, when uncertainty had filled young Daphne's every moment. She was determined to never be so vulnerable again.

But *Grandmaman* grew older and still Daphne wasn't married.

Everything could change in a moment. She

clutched the linens and wished again that her Christmas wish would come true.

It had been a long time since Daphne had vowed to take care of Eurydice forever, and perhaps her sister had forgotten the pledge. Daphne never would.

She had to marry well and soon.

Her wish had seemed to show promise when they'd unexpectedly encountered the Duke of Inverfyre—even more so when he watched her so intently—but his carriage had passed theirs that afternoon and they hadn't seen him again.

Daphne had liked him, too. Surely the opportunity wasn't lost forever?

Jenny's cold had grown steadily worse as they journeyed south and Eurydice had a slight sniffle by the time they arrived. She'd gone to bed early and was still sleeping deeply in the room when Daphne's dream awakened her.

Daphne stared at the ceiling and feared for the future.

She wished she was the clever one.

The one kind of tutelage to which Daphne took naturally was her grandmother's instruction about the management of finances. She had expressed curiosity and her grandmother had explained, apparently thinking that a taste would suffice. But Daphne had been curious and more interested in following the path of money than conjugating German verbs. Their lessons had continued ever since, and it was Daphne who was summoned to help her grandmother with the accounts. She knew the sum of the inheritance left to herself and her sister, and recognized that it was a pittance.

Their grandfather had stipulated in his will that if he pre-deceased his wife, she might remain in the smaller house now known as the dower house for her lifetime. Of course, he had passed away before Daphne had been born, before even her father and heir to the estate had taken a wife. Once *Grandmaman* passed, Daphne and Eurydice would have no home, unless their cousin, the viscount, chose to be charitable in Lady North Barrows' absence.

Daphne would rather be reliant upon a husband than a cousin, and thus she was resolved to marry for both money and title. Her sister thought this was a foolish whim, but it was an utterly practical choice.

Eurydice was right on one account: the title *was* a whim. Daphne didn't truly need to be a duchess. People were more accepting of an ambition to marry a duke than one to wed a wealthy man—and she knew that her grandmother would never permit her to marry an untitled man, independent of his financial situation.

A duke with a fortune it would have to be.

Like the Duke of Inverfyre.

Who had ridden onward, as if he'd forgotten her.

In the night, with uncertainty lingering from her dream, all horrors seemed possible.

Daphne tossed and turned but could not go back to sleep.

At home, she often went to the kitchen after her nightmare.

Her belly growled, as if to encourage the idea.

Daphne rose and donned a robe. She debated the merit of ringing the bell, but knew that Jenny needed her sleep to battle that fearsome cold. She didn't want to awaken Nelson or Eurydice either.

Surely no one would mind if she went to the kitchen here?

Surely it would ease her fears to *do* something, rather than lie abed and fret?

Feeling very bold, she slipped out of their chamber and into the darkened hall. Castle Keyvnor was quiet and cool, filled with shadows. Daphne struck the flint when she was in the corridor and lit the candle she'd brought from the chamber.

The flame blew a little in a draft. Daphne put the flint in her pocket and cupped her hand around the flame, then hurried quietly down the hall.

It seemed the only sound was the rumbling of her stomach. She had a strange sense that she was being watched, which was ridiculous.

Daphne paused at the summit of the stairs, listened and felt her heart skip. Had that been a swishing sound behind her, like the swirling skirt of a taffeta dress?

Of course not. She continued a little more quickly.

A clock chimed somewhere far below her. If it was right, the hour was three in the morning. She retraced their path of earlier in the evening to the foyer, then tried to guess the location of the kitchens. At the end of the corridor on the main floor, there was a smaller door tucked into the corner. It looked as if it led to the servants' quarters, as it was too plain and small to lead anywhere else.

Daphne opened the door with care and discovered another staircase. This one was less ornate, a very functional staircase that led both up and down.

The servants' stairs. The kitchen would be down.

She held her candle high and hurried down the stairs. She could smell roast meat then, soap, herbs, and baking. Her nose led her to the darkened kitchen, which was clean and empty. Banked coals glowed on the hearth and a dog was curled up, sleeping there. Its tail thumped at the sight of her but it didn't abandon its cozy spot.

On one long table, there was a basket with a cloth over it. That was just as Cook left extra baking at home. Daphne lifted the cloth and smiled at the sight of the scones.

Triumph! There were a dozen. She would eat just one. She wouldn't leave a mess.

Daphne reached in just as someone spoke.

"Who are you and what are you doing here?"

The words were uttered softly, but Daphne was still surprised. She jumped, dropped both candle and scone, then spun to face the person who spoke. The candle extinguished itself, then fell out of the holder and rolled. "I am Daphne Goodenham," she confessed, a little breathless. "I was hungry."

A young girl stepped out of the shadows. She was a few years older than Daphne and clearly a maid. "Didn't you ring for your maid?"

"Jenny is sick. I couldn't think to trouble her at this hour."

Her companion seemed to be surprised.

Or suspicious.

"I often go to the kitchen at home. I didn't think it would be any trouble here."

"It's not." The maid nodded toward the basket. "There are plenty left from today, and they'll be making new ones in a few hours." She picked up the candle then set it into the holder again. Daphne used the flint to light it again, and had a better look at her companion. She had curly brown hair and looked to be just as wide awake as Daphne.

She was glad to not be alone.

"I'm Mary," the maid said with a quick smile and a curtsey.

"How pleasant to meet you," Daphne said, thinking it would be rude to eat in front of the other woman. Maybe she'd take the scone back to her room.

"You might as well eat here. I won't tell, and there won't be crumbs in your room, then."

"Thank you."

"Let me get the butter." Mary also poured Daphne a glass of milk. She then stood on the other side of the heavy table.

"It's the middle of the night," Daphne chided, making a gesture of invitation. "You need not stand as if we are at dinner."

Mary smiled and bobbed a curtsey, then took a seat. Daphne pushed the basket of scones toward her and the girl glanced over her shoulder as if fearful of being caught.

"Tell them I had two," Daphne said and Mary took one. The girl ate quietly and Daphne chose to take advantage of the opportunity to learn more. "Can you tell me who has come for the wedding?"

"Certainly. The castle is full of guests and so is Hollybrook Park." Mary ticked off on her fingers. "There's...."

In the long list, she made no mention of the Duke of Inverfyre, much to Daphne's disappointment. Daphne smiled. "What a large and merry wedding it will be, with so many guests come to wish them well."

"And there are more in the village, too."

"Truly? Is there a tavern there, then?"

"Two of them. The Mermaid's Kiss is where the gentry will stay, to be sure. The Crown and Anchor is more for sailors."

Daphne finished her scone, thinking furiously. She was sure the duke had mentioned the Mermaid's Kiss. Could she find a way to see him again? "I'm curious about Bocka Morrow. We didn't have time to visit during Samhain. Isn't there an apothecary's shop I might visit?"

Mary laughed. "There is, and the witches are there."

"Witches?"

"Aye, they make love spells." Mary finished her scone. "But you didn't even ask about the ghosts."

Daphne didn't much care for ghost stories—her recurring nightmare provided sufficient fear—but she knew those at Castle Keyvnor were much taken with their ghosts. "When we were here before, they said there was a young boy, named Paul, who cries in the night."

Mary nodded. "The earl's young son."

"And Baron Tyrell, who killed himself when his beloved Lady Helena wed another. Isn't her portrait in the gallery?" Daphne said, remembering.

Mary's eyes shone. "But now Lord Snow has arrived wearing a ring, called the Grimstone, which banishes the ghosts."

"That I do not believe," Daphne said firmly.

"That's only because you weren't here when he arrived. There was a sound like a crack of lightning and ghosts were cast into the sky."

"Did you see it?"

"I heard about it. My uncle is the groom, and he said there was such a commotion in the stables as you have never seen." Mary's eyes shone. "He told me about the Grimstone, which he never thought was real until he saw it this day." She sobered and sighed. "I can only hope that it doesn't banish Benedict."

She must have been referring to yet another ghost. "Why not?"

"Because I love him, and I could not bear it if we were parted forever."

Although the other woman appeared to be convinced of her tale, Daphne remained skeptical. Ghosts thrown into the sky? If they were banished and thrown anywhere, it would be into the great beyond. She thought it would not be prudent to note that this Benedict was dead and Mary was not, thus they were already parted.

The girl had been kind, after all.

Daphne stood and picked up her candle. "It will be morning soon enough. Thank you for the butter and the conversation. Perhaps I will see you tomorrow."

"Perhaps you will. Have a care on your way back upstairs, my lady," Mary said. "The ghosts are not always friendly at Castle Keyvnor, and after today, they may be very angry indeed."

"I thank you for the warning." Daphne retraced her steps, climbing the servant's stairs to the main floor, thinking that worldly concerns were more worrisome than ghosts.

She peeked around the door at the summit and realized she'd already taken a wrong turn. This wasn't the foyer she recognized. There was a staircase in the shadows ahead, but it was smaller than the one she'd descended.

She looked back down the stairs but it was silent and dark below. Surely she could find her way once she was in the main house? The servant's corridors would be like a maze—that she'd already gone the wrong way meant that she was likely to become even more lost.

She stepped into the corridor and closed the door behind herself. The sole illumination was a shaft of moonlight. A clock chimed the half hour. It sounded like the same clock she'd heard before, but it was more distant. She hurried up the stairs to find that the hall above was lined with closed doors, all of which looked the same.

Was that the little alcove near the room she shared with Eurydice? It was too far away to be certain, but Daphne thought it might be. She hurried toward it, her heart beginning to pound. Instead of being silent, the house also sounded to be full of whispers. She was certain that she heard the swish of taffeta again, the scuttle of mice, the stealthy step of someone following her. She remembered the story of an old wing of the castle being out of use and the whispers that ghosts and madwomen lived there. She thought about ghosts and walked a little more quickly. She glanced over her shoulder but saw no one.

Daphne was sure she heard someone else breathing.

Was it a ghost?

Nonsense! Still, she hastened on.

The alcove wasn't the one she recalled. The corridor bent ahead and Daphne hurried toward the corner. Sanctuary must be just ahead. As she approached the corner, she felt a chill and heard a moan that made the hair stand on the back of her neck. Ghosts! There was a gust of air and her candle was extinguished.

Rather than stopping to light it again, Daphne ran.

She rounded the corner in terror and collided with something too solid to be a ghost. She gasped. A man's hands locked around her shoulders to steady her.

He swore and she had the barest glimpse of his blazing blue eyes before he spun her around so that her back was turned to him. "And a good morning to you, my fair damsel," he said in a low whisper that made Daphne's toes curl.

Her heart raced in shock but he didn't release her. She should have run but she didn't want to be alone again just yet. His grip was strong and the warmth of his hands reassuring.

Who was he? Daphne swallowed, recalling that he had been dressed all in black, a shadow against the darkness. He was taller and broader than her, and she couldn't forget the brilliance of his eyes. She tried to turn to face him again but his grip tightened slightly.

"Haven't you heard that curiosity killed the cat?" he murmured, his breath fanning her ear. Daphne could feel the hard heat of him close behind her and her knees weakened.

"Are you a ghost?" she managed to say and he chuckled.

"Not yet. Are you?"

She shook her head and felt his hand slide over her shoulder in a caress. She glanced down and watched his fingers. Even with his black leather glove, she could see that his hands were long and elegant, strong hands. To her astonishment, he lifted a tendril of her hair and let it slide through his gloved fingers, the blond curl gleaming against the black leather.

"Maybe you're just a dream," he whispered. "Sadly, there is only one way to be certain."

Daphne didn't know who he was or why he was there, but she didn't care. This was the stuff of the novels she and Eurydice devoured! "How will you discover the truth?" she asked lightly.

"With a kiss, of course," he replied without hesitation. Perhaps he read those same stories. "Every disreputable vision or ghost is dispelled by a kiss."

"Sirens dissolve with a kiss," Daphne agreed.

"Indeed." His voice rumbled low, awakening a yearning within Daphne. He still held her shoulders, his thumbs caressing her through her robe. She thought of those eyes, that barest glimpse of a square jaw, and swallowed.

"A fine suggestion," she said boldly, keeping her voice low. "For I should like to be certain that you are no apparition, sir." She heard him catch his breath in surprise, then his lips were against her ear.

"Close your eyes, my temptress," he murmured.

Daphne did as he requested and without delay. "Done." She was immediately spun in place, and the weight of one gloved hand slid around her nape. His other hand was on the back of her waist, drawing her close. She felt him lean closer and her breasts collided with his hard chest. She could have run. She could have twisted out of his embrace. She could have opened her eyes. He granted her the time to be certain.

But it was far too perfect to be kissed by a handsome stranger in the dark, when no one else would ever know. It was a delicious secret, one to be held between herself and this man of mystery, and Daphne couldn't resist the invitation to know more.

"You promised me a kiss, sir," she dared to whisper. She rose to her toes and put her hands on his shoulders, keeping her eyes closed as she parted her lips in invitation.

She didn't have to wait long for him to accept.

What was the delightful Miss Goodenham doing, wandering the corridors of Castle Keyvnor in the early hours of the morning? Alexander didn't know and as soon as she collided with him, he didn't care. She smelled seductively feminine. She wore only a chemise and a robe, and when his hands closed over her shoulders to steady her, he felt an overwhelming urge to draw her into his embrace. That she smelled so sweet, that she wore so little, that her hair was in a loose braid, that it was dark and they were alone, made the encounter enticingly intimate.

As if he had come to her in her bedchamber.

Alexander couldn't dismiss that notion, not once he had touched her.

Had she seen his features? He couldn't imagine that she had had time to recognize him, especially as she'd only seen him before in his disguise. It was a mercy that he had used his foolish voice at the tavern, for he had spoken in his own usual tones when he addressed her in the night, too surprised to disguise his voice.

He should have released her. He should have frightened her. He should have let her flee. He gave her the opportunity, despite his desires, because he was a gentleman—even if on this particular night, he played the role of a thief.

But she welcomed his kiss. It was a invitation he couldn't deny.

One kiss.

Alexander knew it couldn't be a chaste kiss, not when Miss Goodenham's lips softened beneath his and she leaned against him. He caught her closer and deepened his kiss before he could think twice about the wisdom of that, and when she melted against him in surrender, he locked his arms around her, crushing her against his chest. She wasn't afraid, though, but seemed to welcome his tutelage. She mimicked his movements, sliding one hand around his neck and one around his waist, just as he held her, meeting him touch for touch. The kiss heated his blood and made him yearn for more.

More than was his right to take, even if she was impulsive enough to give it.

A clock chimed the quarter hour, recalling Alexander to his senses. He broke the kiss with reluctance, gazed upon her flushed cheeks, then drew his hood over his head to shadow his features. He stepped back when her lashes fluttered, then touched his finger to the tip of her nose.

"A siren after all," he murmured, his voice husky. He watched her smile. "But you must not see me. I was no more than a shadow in the night."

"But..."

He dropped his finger to her lips and couldn't resist the urge to slide it across them. She shivered, so responsive that he felt a fool for stepping away from her. "Not a word, my siren. You did not see me. We did not meet. You will return to your chamber and have sweet dreams, your reputation intact."

"I will dream of a specter in the night," she agreed. "Whose kiss is a dangerous temptation."

Alexander smiled. "Keep your eyes closed," he whispered. "I will fetch your candle."

"I have a flint in my pocket," she said.

"Then you can relight it once I am gone." He retrieved the candle and restored it to the candlestick she'd dropped, then placed the candlestick in her hand. He leaned closer, unable to resist touching his lips to her cheek once more. "Count to twenty before you open your eyes," he murmured.

"Aye, sir," she agreed, her lips curving in a smile that invited his touch.

Alexander surveyed her once more, knowing he would recall this vision often. "Sleep well, my siren."

"And you, sir," she whispered, then began to count.

Alexander did not delay. He fled on silent feet, ensuring there was no sign of him before she finished her count.

Before he had even left Castle Keyvnor—slipping out the unlocked window in the library, just as he had entered the castle—his decision was made. He would definitely go to London for the season, journeying there directly from Cornwall. He could not tolerate the notion of his innocent seductress being claimed by another man.

Back in his room at the inn, his arrival unobserved, Alexander removed the seed that Anthea had given him and once again rolled it between his finger and thumb. He could not deny that it had swollen a bit, a young root pushing against the shell from the inside.

The story was whimsy.

It was nonsense.

It was time to know for certain. He put water in the glass from his wine then dropped the seed into it, watching it sink to the bottom and roll to one side. He set the glass before the fire, having no expectations, and finally got himself to bed.

"Where were you?" Eurydice said the next morning as Daphne was getting dressed. Eurydice was lacing Daphne's stays since Jenny was staying downstairs for the day. Her cold had gotten much worse and *Grandmaman* had insisted. Nelson was with *Grandmaman* and Daphne was too impatient to wait.

But without her stays laced, Daphne couldn't escape her sister's questions.

She was sure Eurydice had planned it that way.

Daphne felt as if the entire world would know at a glimpse that she'd kissed a stranger in the night—or that she'd thought about him incessantly ever since—but was determined to keep her promise to that man. "Whatever do you mean?"

"I woke up in the middle of the night and you were gone. A clock was striking three."

"I was hungry. I went down to the kitchen."

"You should have rung for Jenny."

"I didn't want to wake her up for the sake of a scone."

"You were gone a long time," Eurydice said, showing the annoying persistence that was typical of her. Sometimes Daphne thought her sister could smell a secret and then she was like their grandmother's terrier, reluctant to leave the matter until she'd unearthed the prize.

Daphne gave her sister an exasperated look. "I got lost. This castle is enormous." It wasn't precisely a lie.

Eurydice rolled her eyes. "It's not that complicated."

"Well, maybe I'm not that clever," Daphne replied.

"Did you find the kitchen? Or did you just give up and come back here?"

"I found it. And there were some leftover scones from tea. I met Mary who told me a story about a magical ring."

Eurydice perched on the bed to listen. "Here?"

"Of course, here! One of the gentlemen, Lord Snow, wears it and it's supposed to banish ghosts."

Eurydice smiled. "If it's true, the ring will have plenty of chances to do that here."

"I thought it foolish, but Mary said ghosts were thrown into the sky on his arrival yesterday." Daphne put on her shoes and considered her reflection in the mirror. "You made these curls very nicely," she said, admiring her sister's handwork.

"You did mine better."

"But I enjoy it. You hate doing it, though you are improving."

"I took especial care as doubtless you intend to talk to the duke again."

To be sure, the duke offered a little less temptation on this day than he had at the tavern. Was it conceivable that such a man, however rich he might be, would be able to kiss her as the stranger in the night had done? Daphne had tingled in a most pleasurable way. Indeed, just thinking about that kiss—and the intensity of his blue eyes—made her flush all over again.

But then, the duke had blue eyes and an intense gaze as well.

How curious.

Daphne smiled because her sister was watching her. "And here I thought you were considering a post as a lady's maid, since *Grandmaman* has forbidden you to become a governess."

They laughed together.

"And perhaps you don't really wish to meet this particular duke again. Goodness, Daphne, but he reminds me of Falstaff."

Daphne frowned as they left their chamber together. "In that play *Grandmaman* took us to see in London?"

Eurydice nodded. "*Henry IV*. Falstaff was so fat. I couldn't believe that any man could be that large and still manage to walk, but your duke proves it can be so."

"I can't remember that actor's name," Daphne said, recalling another detail. "We scarce recognized him when we saw him in town."

Eurydice laughed. "The power of disguise. Come along. I'm famished, probably because I didn't have a scone in the middle of the night. Let us have something to eat before we walk to Bocka Morrow for church."

Daphne slanted a glance at her sister. "You just want to tease me about the duke."

"I just want to see you realize your mistake. I don't think you will like him nearly as well on second acquaintance. He is a fool, Daphne, and not a man who will ever hold your heart."

Daphne didn't reply. She was thinking about the handsome stranger and wondering what she would say to him if they met again at breakfast. Her heart skipped at the prospect. Would he look as dashing in the daylight as at night? Would she recognize him?

And what was he doing, abroad in the middle of the night? She'd never asked and only wondered in the morning if his kiss had been a way to keep her from doing as much.

He might well be a scoundrel or a rake.

Then she thought of the duke, his fine legs and the intense glitter of his eyes. Could it be that he and the actor who had played Falstaff had a disguise in common?

Or had she become as whimsical as the maid Mary after her midnight adventure?

CHAPTER THREE

Alexander awakened to find that a lush plant growing from his wine glass. Surely, his eyes deceived him. That small seed couldn't have grown so much in a few hours!

He rubbed his eyes and rose to examine the plant, but it was no illusion. He could see its roots coiled inside the cup, and it had grown a vine of at least a foot long, one adorned with fleshy dark leaves. There was even a bud tucked beneath one leaf.

Rupert was suitably astonished by the sight of it, but Alexander didn't explain. He didn't think the truth would sound plausible.

He halfway didn't believe it himself. Could Anthea have been right about the old tale and the vine's habit of growing when the laird courted a wife?

If so, he knew which lady he would court. Miss Goodenham was the most captivating girl he'd met in years.

As he dressed, he considered that he scarcely knew her.

He recalled how he relied upon his instincts in all other matters and wondered whether to trust them in this one.

When the bells rang for church at St. David's, the bud burst into a blossom. Alexander could almost hear the petals unfurling. They were as red as blood and the flower was as wide as his palm. Rupert swore and took a step away from the vine. Alexander could only take its blooming as a sign. He plucked the deep red flower and tucked it into his buttonhole.

It had a most enchanting perfume, and one deep breath of it reminded him of the fire in a certain damsel's kiss.

❧

There was no man at breakfast who might have been the mysterious stranger Daphne had met in the night. The gentlemen were fine, but not a one was the right height and breadth, had the right hands or the same wondrous blue eyes. None of them gave her more than a passing glance.

Who was he?

Where was he? Daphne supposed he could have been a servant or another guest who had not yet come down for breakfast. What had he been doing in the corridor at such an hour? The more she considered it, the more details she recalled. He had been dressed all in black, but he hadn't worn a nightshirt. No, he had been dressed in breeches and boots, with a great cloak.

Had he been an intruder?

No one mentioned a theft or other villainous deed, which puzzled Daphne even more.

Why had her mysterious man been within Castle Keyvnor?

The conversation in the dining room was interrupted by a man's hearty laugh in the foyer. All the women at the table looked up, particularly when he was greeted by the Earl of Bansfield. "Young Nathaniel! I hope you slept well!"

"I did, thank you, cousin. I trust that Lady Tamsyn is pleased?"

The earl laughed. "She is delighted."

"Then my mission is complete. I shall ride for home this morning."

"But you cannot reach London before Christmas, Nathaniel," the earl said. "Surely you will stay for the wedding?"

"I would not be so presumptuous. I know I am not expected to linger..."

"But I have ensured there is a chamber for you all the same," the earl said heartily. "We cannot send you from the doors at Christmas!"

"I thank you kindly, sir."

The earl entered the dining room with a young man who smiled at the gathered company.

"My wife's second cousin, Nathaniel Cushing, for those of you who did not meet him yesterday," the earl said. "Surely you know everyone here, Nathaniel?"

"Those I do not I will meet soon enough." Mr. Cushing bowed to the earl. "Thank you again for your generosity, sir." The earl nodded and departed, and the new arrival helped himself to breakfast.

Daphne took the opportunity to study him. Nathaniel Cushing was about a decade older than herself. He had dark hair and was both fiercely handsome and elegantly dressed. He appeared to be a most genial individual. He heaped a plate from the sideboard then took a place beside Daphne, introducing himself before he sat down.

He could have been the man she had encountered the night before. He looked suitably dashing, to be sure, and bold enough to have demanded a kiss in the night. But when he bestowed a warm smile upon her, his gaze lingering with appreciation, she noticed that his eyes were brown, not blue.

He had not been the one to kiss her, of that she was certain.

"What a marvel this place is," he said with enthusiasm. "Have you been here before?"

"Once. This autumn we visited briefly."

"How fortunate for you, Miss Goodenham. Perhaps I might prevail upon you to give me a short tour?"

"I mean to attend church this morning, Mr.

Cushing. It would have to wait until after lunch."

"That would be marvelous. What better than a walk on a Sunday afternoon?"

"Cushing, do you know what Great Uncle Timothy sent to Lady Tamsyn?" asked another guest from down the table. It was one of the gentlemen.

"I would wager it is a gem," Mr. Cushing said. "Though I could not imagine which one. When I make a delivery for my great uncle, the box is sealed and locked before it is given to me. The key is dispatched separately to the recipient."

"But surely someone could steal the box?" Daphne asked.

Mr. Cushing's manner turned grim. "They would have to kill me first," he vowed.

"Indeed?"

"Indeed. My uncle entrusts me with these tasks and I would never fail him." He winked at Daphne and tucked into his eggs. "Beggars cannot be choosers and poor relations must earn their own way. I do quite like being Uncle Timothy's runner, though."

"Why is that?"

"I see the most wondrous places." He gestured with his fork. "I should never be invited to such a place as Castle Keyvnor at Christmas, much less have the opportunity to meet so many people throughout the year. His gifts give me purpose and adventure. I hope he never runs out of gems to give away."

"Does he often give gems away?"

"He is a collector of some renown, and has neither wife nor children. As he ages, he seems more inclined to bestow fine gifts on others. It is a mark of his splendid character."

"He might honor you with such a gift, surely?" Daphne suggested.

Mr. Cushing laughed easily, as if he had never given the notion any consideration. "But why? If he made me rich, he might lose me as a servant. Indeed, I might decline such a gift if it meant surrendering the opportunity to meet ladies like you, Miss Goodenham." He smiled at her, his eyes twinkling merrily, and Daphne could not help but be flattered by his attentions.

He had admitted he was penniless. He certainly had no title. Encouraging his attentions would do naught in the achievement of her goal to ensure the future of herself and Eurydice.

Daphne smiled, then excused herself. She did not want to be late for church, lest she miss a glimpse of the duke, and she did not want to walk to Bocka Morrow with Nathaniel Cushing, lest his presence keep the duke from speaking to her.

Her grandmother had taught her much of choosing practicality over romance.

Miss Goodenham came to church.

Alexander hid his smile behind the gesture of taking a pinch of snuff, for he was absurdly glad to see her. He watched as she surveyed the congregation and noted that her gaze lingered upon him. His smile broadened that it was admiration lighting her gaze and not revulsion.

Yet he had chosen this hideous outfit of mauve and silver to appall one and all. Even the red flower clashed.

Perhaps the lady had bad taste.

Or perhaps she was sufficiently perceptive to see beyond illusion to the truth. As if to reinforce that notion, she smiled prettily when their gazes met, then seated herself with her cousins.

How could he determine how trustworthy she was? Anthea had hit the mark when she suggested he wed an honest woman. The trick was to find one.

Perhaps he could charm a dinner invitation from the family. It would give him both the opportunity to observe Nathaniel Cushing and to learn more about Miss Goodenham.

Before the bells of St. David's had finished their merry pealing after the service, Alexander was expected at eight at Castle Keyvnor for dinner. Miss Goodenham's pleasure in the news was unmistakable.

"What a marvelous buttonhole you have today, Your Grace," she said, then leaned closer to sniff the flower. Her eyes widened and he wondered if its perfume sent the same surge of desire through her.

Her gaze dropped to his lips and parted slightly, even as she flushed.

He recalled the sweetness of her kiss and wanted

another.

"Wherever did you find it?"

"Ah, I could never tell!" he said with a giggle. "A man must keep some secrets to himself."

"As must a lady," she agreed. "Secrets, do you not think, add a wondrous spice to any exchange?"

"Secrets," he agreed, "sift the observant from those less so."

Her smile was radiant. "I see we are of one mind in this. Do you ever attend the theater, Your Grace?"

Her cousins were heading for the castle and her sister gave her a glare, but Miss Goodenham lingered. Alexander offered his elbow to her to escort her a bit of the way, and she accepted with a smile. She leaned against him a little so he could feel the curve of her breast against his arm.

"The theater?" he echoed, raising his quizzing glass to examine her. She was utterly perfect. "I do. And you?"

"Oh, not very often, but I did see a Shakespearean play the last time we were in London." Her smile was impish. "*Grandmaman* took us to see *Henry IV*."

"Perhaps she thought it a good way for you to learn more of border politics."

"Perhaps, though it would have been a more compelling lesson if she had not fallen asleep herself."

Alexander chuckled.

"I should have preferred to have seen something

more amusing."

"Which of the plays would you have favored?"

She cast him a knowing glance. "*Twelfth Night* is my favorite, Your Grace."

"Because love conquers all?"

"You sound like my sister!"

"And mine, to be sure. But that is not your reasoning?"

She frowned. "I should like to think love would be triumphant, Your Grace, but find it easier to believe that justice will prevail." She met his gaze. "It is a more reassuring notion, do you not think?"

"I do."

"Plus I find characters in disguise most beguiling."

Alexander's heart stopped, then leaped. "But surely it is implausible for people to so readily err in identification?"

"I do not think so. Few people truly look or pay attention. And people pretend to be other than they are all the time. Some simply do it better than others."

"Does that make them dishonest?"

"Not if they have good cause. I am certain, for example, Your Grace, that if you or I ever donned a disguise, it would be for only the very best reasons."

"And how might you be so certain of that?"

She smiled sunnily. "My heart tells me so, and I trust it implicitly." She continued, not giving him a chance to reply, "But what I most remember from that play was Falstaff."

"A rogue and a scoundrel."

"To be sure, and a very fat one, at least upon the stage." Her gaze dropped to his belly and he had the sudden suspicion that she had seen through his ruse. "Your waistcoat is most splendid today, Your Grace," she said lightly. "I have never seen such lavish embroidery."

"For church, you know. Lord knows one must wear one's best."

"Indeed. This silvery shade of mauve is most attractive. What do you call it?"

"*Lavande*, of course."

"Of course. Lavendar. And the grey?"

"*Argent.*"

"Oh, no, sir, it cannot be *argent*. *Argent* is darker, like the spots on a dappled horse." She bit her lip and surveyed his waistcoat, which was filled with such bulk that it had required a considerable measure of cloth. Then she smiled. "It is the color of a dove. *Gris tourterelle.*"

He simpered, to disguise how thoroughly he was charmed. "Everything sounds so much better in French, don't you think?"

"I do!" She laughed up at him. "While it sounds worse in German."

"More earthy, to be sure."

"I also think that your inspiration will cost *Grandmaman* a fortune once we reach London. Why, each suit you wear makes me wish for a dress in the same combination, Your Grace. Imagine a dress in this *lavande*, embellished with silver beads. It would be like moonlight."

He could imagine her in just such a dress, with his mother's amethysts. Daphne Goodenham would look like a goddess who had set foot on the earth. "It would be magnificent," he agreed. "With slippers of silver silk to match."

She laughed. "You would be perilous to a dressmaker's budget, Your Grace."

"So my sister has often said."

"You mentioned before that you had a sister. Will you tell me of her?"

"She is younger than me by a few years. Anthea is her name."

Daphne looked up at him, her expression sober. "You are very fond of her. I hear it in your words."

"Indeed. She is the sweetest of ladies."

"Has she had her debut?"

Alexander frowned despite himself. "It did not proceed well, despite my best efforts. Her heart was broken, and now she remains at Airdfinnan. No amount of cajoling will convince her to leave."

"How sad! Since you have said you frequent Town, it must be lonely there."

"She insists she prefers solitude."

"But she will never find a man of merit or fall in love so long as she remains secluded."

"You think I should compel her to leave her sanctuary?"

"No, no, Your Grace. I think it is a fine and noble thing that you offer her a haven, and that you defend her desire." Miss Goodenham frowned a little. "But it is so much easier when a beloved sister desires something that will make her happy in the end."

"Might I assume that you refer to Miss Eurydice?"

"I do. She thinks she does not need to wed, or that she can marry for love independent of fortune." The lady shook her head so that her blond curls danced. "It is whimsy, Your Grace. Women like us must be practical."

He was intrigued. "Women like you?"

"My sister and I were orphaned nine years ago, when our parents both died in an accident. We were very fortunate that *Grandmaman* saw fit not only to take us into her home, but to see us educated. She even intends to give us each a season."

"But surely you are her only granddaughters."

"We are, but her fortune is not infinite and she is of an age that I rather imagine she would prefer to be left to her letters and her gardens. The fact remains that she grows older." She lifted her chin, looking valiant and wise. "When our parents died, *Grandmaman* was in Bath. It took a fortnight for her to hear the news and come for us. I will never forget feeling responsible for Eurydice, that we two had only each other in the world. I vowed then that I would ensure our futures myself with a good marriage."

She must have been very young. It clearly had been a frightening experience.

"Eurydice thinks I wish to wed a duke because I

am a frivolous fool," she said with a little smile.

"Perhaps you are not so frivolous as that."

"I do like clothes and I like parties and I suspect I could love a man simply because he granted me the security I desire most. Does that mean I am frivolous?"

"Not entirely so."

"I also like to balance the accounts with *Grandmaman* and ensure that every penny ends up where it belongs."

Alexander was impressed. "That is not frivolous!"

She smiled fleetingly. "Eurydice will wed for passion or not at all, so I must be the one to see that she always has a sanctuary." She glanced up at him. "I suppose that might sound conniving."

"It sounds sensible to me," Alexander acknowledged, forgetting to use his foppish voice. "And it is most admirable that your love for your sister takes such expression." He smiled. "I do not doubt that if you bent your will upon it, you could make any man happy indeed."

"I hope so, Your Grace. I am not as clever as Eurydice, that much is certain."

"But neither are you a fool, my dear."

"No," she agreed, casting him a glance of such mischief that the sight fairly stole Alexander's breath away. "If I may be so bold as to say so, Your Grace, you have the bluest eyes I have ever seen."

"I favor my mother in that, to be sure."

Her gaze dropped to his lips and lingered there,

a flush staining her cheeks. Alexander halted and made a show of being out of breath, then doffed his glove to take a pinch of snuff. She watched his hands avidly, a conviction dawning in her eyes.

"Are you ever restless at night, Your Grace?" she asked and Alexander's heart stopped cold.

"Nay, never!" he lied, taking a hearty tone. "My valet says I snore fit to wake the dead!" He giggled again, but her gaze did not waver.

"How fortunate you are." Her cousins called and she glanced toward them, then curtseyed before him. "I shall look forward to seeing you at dinner tonight, Your Grace." Her eyes danced. "I cannot wait to see what you will wear!"

Alexander laughed, trying to turn the sound into a chortle.

"Miss Goodenham!" a man cried and Alexander sobered at the sight of his prey. Nathaniel Cushing swept in beside the girl and took her arm with such confidence that Alexander longed to challenge him. "The finest prize in the company will be left behind and I cannot permit it to be so."

Daphne's gaze clung to Alexander's for a moment and he wondered what she saw. "I do not mean to be left behind," she said lightly, putting a bit of distance between herself and Nathaniel. "It is a beautiful day and there is yet some time before luncheon."

"But I desire every moment with you," Cushing insisted. "For there is no greater beauty at Castle Keyvnor this Christmas."

Alexander did not hear Miss Goodenham's reply but he watched her depart, wondering all the while at the perils of her guessing his secret. She had guessed. He was certain of it and the notion was terrifying.

Surely she could not cost him the prize?

The duke *was* the intruder. His eyes were just as blue. His lips were just as firm. Despite his paunch, his face was lean. His hands were long and strong, just like those of the intruder, and his legs were muscled. The duke used a similar disguise as the actor playing Falstaff, though apparently only Daphne had pierced the veil of his illusion.

The realization only redoubled her determination to win him. She was certain he had good reason for his disguise. He defended his sister, which was ample measure of his noble character, and his kiss nearly melted her bones. That he was a duke was as icing on the cake.

The Duke of Inverfyre was perfect.

She fancied that she was not the sole one who felt the attraction. The hungry blue glance he gave her at intervals was utterly out of character with his foppish guise, and reminded her all too well of his kiss.

The look he had given Mr. Cushing for interrupting had been pure fire.

The sight had sent heat through her, as well.

Daphne could not wait to see him again. She

managed to separate herself from Mr. Cushing upon arrival at the castle as there was word that *Grandmaman* was coming down with Jenny's cold. She had remained in her rooms and resented the lack of news. She demanded to know who had gone to the village.

"Nathaniel Cushing," she said with disdain, then punctuated the words with a sneeze. "A ne'er-do-well if ever there was."

"Anyone with sense can see with a glance that he's a rake and a scoundrel," Eurydice agreed and her grandmother beamed at her.

"Anyone," Daphne agreed.

"I'm surprised you don't like him," Eurydice said. "He's handsome and charming, after all."

Daphne shrugged. "I don't."

"Because he's not rich," Eurydice said.

"How could you know such a thing?"

"When you were walking with the duke, our cousins were gossiping. They said he has nothing to his name but debt. He's something of a black sheep."

"But the earl expected him. Mr. Cushing must have had some reason for coming," Daphne said. "In fact, I believe he acted as a courier for his uncle, Mr. Timothy Cushing."

"Maybe he means to steal the Eye of India!" Eurydice declared.

Grandmaman snorted, then sneezed again. "From what I hear, he must have come to ask for money. Or a rich wife." She peered at Daphne. "Don't let him lead you astray, my dear, tempting you under the mistletoe or kissing you in the moonlight."

"Daphne has no money," Eurydice contributed. "Perhaps she won't tempt him."

"Any man might be tempted by Daphne, even if he couldn't do anything honorable about it," her grandmother corrected sternly. "I will not have scandal over a man like Nathaniel Cushing. Am I understood?"

"Yes, *Grandmaman*," Daphne and Eurydice agreed in unison.

What about a scandal over a man like the Duke of Inverfyre? Daphne didn't ask, but counted the moments until dinner.

"Now tell me," their grandmother demanded. "Just how richly was the church decorated for the holidays? I hope there was holly and a fine Advent wreath..."

❦

"I'm not certain you would be wise to sleep in this chamber," Rupert said with some aggravation. "That wretched vine might completely engulf you during the night."

Alexander stared at the plant in question. While he had been at church, the plant had grown with astonishing speed. It was the size of a small shrub, both growing upright and trailing over the table. It was covered in deep red blooms and the scent of it was dizzying. Rupert had opened the window, admitting a damp chill, but the plant did not wilt.

Alexander thought of Daphne, the suspicion that she had pierced his disguise, and let admiration fill his heart.

The plant grew before his very eyes.

Rupert swore with enthusiasm. "I should chuck it out!"

"Not until my quest is complete."

"I fail to see what this infestation has to do with springing the trap."

Alexander knotted his cravat with care, declining to tell Rupert that he referred to another quest altogether. He liked the scent of the red flowers. The perfume seemed to lighten his heart, and optimism was a fine asset.

Miss Goodenham *had* admired his buttonhole. He took a fresh flower and a bud, twining them with several leaves to make a more elaborate buttonhole for dinner. He then turned and flaunted his splendor for Rupert, who shuddered.

"You are a vision that will be impossible to forget, Your Grace."

"Indeed."

Rupert brushed the shoulders of Alexander's silk brocade coat. "Are you certain Lady Tamsyn has received the gem?"

"Yes. I hope she will wear it at dinner, as Mr. Timothy Cushing requested."

"Surely the villain will not attempt anything more than admiration before the household?"

"Surely not." Alexander met Rupert's gaze in the mirror. "The sooner it has been admired, the sooner he will steal it. And then we shall finally discover how he removes his prize from the house."

"He has never been caught with the stolen gems on his person, no matter how thoroughly house and guests are searched."

"Never. But mark my words, the Eye of India will be his undoing."

CHAPTER FOUR

Daphne was doomed to disappointment when she reached the dining room, due to the order of precedence and the vast size of the party at dinner. The duke might as well have dined in Bocka Morrow, for all her opportunity to speak with him. He was at the head of the table, which at least meant she could observe him from her place near the other end, but she couldn't even hear his words.

Mr. Cushing paused beside her and granted her an engaging grin. Daphne returned his smile politely. "What good fortune is mine," he said gallantly, sweeping into the seat beside her.

"I could argue that it is mine," Daphne replied in kind, though her heart was not in the words. She might have said something else, but Mr. Cushing suddenly leaned forward.

"I say! Is that the legendary Eye of India, Tamsyn?" he fairly shouted, peering down the table at one of the brides-to-be.

"It is, Nathaniel." Lady Tamsyn's hand rose to touch the brooch. "Great uncle Timothy sent it to me as a wedding gift. He said it belonged in the coffers of the Earl of Banfield and since I'm oldest, it should be mine."

"Is he truly our uncle?" asked Lady Morgan.

"Technically, he's probably a cousin," said Lady Rose.

"Or a great uncle," Lady Morgan suggested.

"I thought he was dead," confided Lady Gwyn, raising a horrified hand to her lips.

"We should have heard if he was," jested Lady Marjorie. "There would have been a ruckus when his gem collection was sold or given in bequests."

Daphne couldn't help but stare at the brooch. She'd never seen such a splendid piece of jewelry. In its center was an enormous sapphire of clear deep blue. The stone was surrounded by swirls of silver, each jammed with sparkling clear gems. It caught the light and glittered.

Surely those stones couldn't all be diamonds?

It would be worth a fortune, then.

"What a handsome gift," Daphne said.

"It is!" Lady Tamsyn said. "I was so surprised."

"I'm glad he sent it to you instead of me," Lady Morgan said. "I should be terrified that it would be stolen."

"Oh, it won't be," Lady Tamsyn said lightly.

"Not here at Castle Keyvnor." She smiled at her betrothed. "And after the holidays, Gryffyn will take it to Lancarrow to be locked up for safekeeping."

"You won't be wearing it daily, after all," he replied with a teasing smile.

"Only until the wedding. Uncle Timothy asked me to wear it for luck until then. It seemed the least I could do."

"Although we have no need of luck," her beloved agreed.

The pair beamed at each other, so happy that they evidently had forgotten every other soul in the room. Daphne knew that she herself had too many expectations of a suitor to hope for love, as well.

She might hope for desire, perhaps.

Respect.

She spared a glance down the table to the duke, flushing when she realized he was watching her. His expression was serious and his eyes vehemently blue.

Then he lifted his quizzing glance and spoke in that falsely high voice. "Upon my word, *there* is a gem!" Evidently not satisfied with the view, he rose from his seat and trotted down the side of the table to Lady Tamsyn's side. He peered at it. "What a marvel! Do you know that the Prince Regent himself has a brooch similar to this, but admittedly somewhat smaller, that he often wears in his cravat?"

"I didn't know that," Lady Tamsyn said. "Although I wouldn't be surprised."

The duke gazed at the gem, nodding to himself. "A prize, to be sure." He flicked a glance across the table. "Do you not agree, Miss Goodenham?"

She colored more deeply to be so singled out. "I have never seen the like, Your Grace, although my experience of gems is limited."

"Marry well, my dear, and that may change," he replied jovially, then winked at her. Daphne blushed as Mr. Cushing chuckled.

"There is sound advice," he murmured.

Meanwhile, the duke took another look. "A magnificent sapphire," he pronounced, then returned to his seat, his heels clicking as he walked.

"But why is it called the Eye of India?" Daphne asked.

"Oh, it has a painting beneath the sapphire, of a man's eye," Mr. Cushing said.

Lady Tamsyn leaned across the table and Daphne could just barely glimpse the eye. "Great Uncle Timothy wrote that it was a gift from a gentleman to his lady love, as a token of his undying affection."

"But we don't know who he was," Lady Morgan added.

"Or the lady, for that matter," Lady Tamsyn agreed. "It is a lovely romantic story, but one that leaves as many questions as answers."

"Such as how Great Uncle Timothy came by it in the first place," Lady Morgan agreed.

Mr. Cushing cleared his throat. "I expect he bought it," he said. "My uncle buys a great many gems, and not always at public auctions. There are many jewelers who know of his collection."

"There you are, Tamsyn," Gryffyn said. "Lord Timothy has ensured your future, for you could always sell the brooch if need be."

Lady Tamsyn laughed prettily, for her future was clearly in no doubt given her betrothed's wealth.

Mr. Cushing cleared his throat. "I would venture to suggest that the man in question might be suspected to have been a Hambly for Uncle Timothy to believe the Eye of India belonged in your possession."

"How perfectly scandalous!" Lady Tamsyn said. "Who do you think it might have been?"

They laughed lightly and began to speculate as the soup was brought in.

After the soup had been served, Mr. Cushing leaned toward her. "I'm not surprised that the duke had a good look at the Eye of India."

"Indeed? Is he reputed to have a taste for gems, like your uncle?"

"More than a taste, to be sure. There is said to be an avarice for them in his family."

"Truly?"

"Truly. His sister Anthea was accused of being a thief and banished from polite society as a result."

"Oh! How horrible."

"It was horrible." Mr. Cushing shook his head. "In her debut season, as well."

"What a ghastly thing. Was she guilty?"

"What do you mean?"

"Well, you said she was accused, not discovered to be guilty. It's not quite the same thing."

He smiled at her indulgently, as if she were a child. "You take the side of a stranger?"

"If it was her debut, I can't imagine she would be scheming to steal gems. She would be too busy thinking about dance cards and eligible beaus and dresses."

Mr. Cushing seemed to find this a foolish view. "Nonetheless, she was accused and fled London for Scotland. Surely no one innocent would have done as much? That she would hurry home and never leave again indicates her guilt."

Daphne could well imagine that the duke's sister might have left the city out of mortification, even at being so accused, not necessarily of guilt. "And was the gem found?"

"No, but then they didn't look at Airdfinnan." Mr. Cushing nodded down the table. "The duke would not let anyone through the gates to search. Perhaps he knows where it is."

"I think it admirable that he defended his sister against rumor and innuendo," Daphne said primly. She rather imagined that the duke might fight dragons for his sister and admired him for that.

"It was not admirable if she was guilty. To harbor a thief is reprehensible." Mr. Cushing shook his head. "And one does wonder how he comes by such wealth. It is said that he doesn't owe so much as a shilling to any man."

Daphne straightened, finding much to admire in

fiscal responsibility and knowing that it did not necessarily mean the duke funded his purchases with theft. She chose not to share her grandmother's comment about the family declining to gamble.

"Is that so uncommon, then?" she asked, feigning ignorance of such matters.

Mr. Cushing gave a bark of a laugh. "To me, it seems a miracle."

Yes, he might be the sort of man to live far beyond his own means. She smiled and ended the conversation, then turned to the cousin on her other side to ask about the wedding preparations.

Daphne was not certain what awakened her.

For once, it wasn't her nightmare.

It was the middle of the night, the room still dark. Eurydice snored, her breath rattling as if she too would take Jenny's cold. That clock chimed in the distance.

Three in the morning again, but this time, Daphne was not hungry.

She felt rather than saw that there was another presence in the room. She couldn't have named what alerted her to the intruder, a faint scent of cologne, perhaps, or a rustle of cloth. She kept her eyes closed, rolled over with a sigh and breathed as if she were asleep.

She heard a footfall. Was it the duke? Even if he was the intruder, surely he was too honorable to assault a girl in her own room? Daphne was prepared to scream if a finger was laid upon her, even as she doubted her duke would act in such a way.

She heard a click, like the closing of her trunk. She opened her eyes slightly and saw a wedge of moonlight as the door to the corridor was opened. She had the barest glimpse of a shadow passing through the door, then the door was closed and there was only the sound of Eurydice's breathing.

Who had been in their room?

Why?

Daphne waited until first light because she didn't want to light a candle and risk awakening Eurydice. She slipped from her bed as quietly as possible and went to her trunk. It looked just as it had the night before and she wondered if she had dreamed of the intruder. She quietly opened her trunk and surveyed the contents in the dim light, then patted the folded chemises and petticoats.

Her hand stilled over a hard shape that hadn't been there before.

It was an unfamiliar drawstring bag, made of deep blue velvet. Daphne's mouth went dry. She cast a glance at Eurydice, then opened the bag, tipping its contents into her hand.

It was the Eye of India.

Panic rose hot in her chest as she stared at the gem.

What should she do?

Daphne recalled Mr. Cushing's tale of the night

before and knew that she could not let herself be named as a thief. Who would believe her if she said someone had placed it in her room? Would she be falsely accused and banished from polite society, like the duke's sister? Daphne could not bear it.

She could not risk it.

Not if she was to guarantee Eurydice's future.

Daphne returned the brooch in its velvet bag and knotted the cord, just as it had been, then replaced it in her trunk. She went back to bed, her thoughts spinning. The others would be awakening. The loss would be discovered. What should she do? If there was a search for the gem, she didn't want to have it with her. Neither did she want it to be found in her possessions.

She wished she could talk to the duke and seek his advice, but it was impossible for her to get to Bocka Morrow without being observed.

Or was it?

No one had seen Jenny since their arrival.

It was not even dawn.

Did she dare? Daphne rang for her maid before she could question her impulse.

One thing was certain: the duke would know what to do.

It was Alexander's custom to rise early in the morning, and travel did not change his routine. It was before dawn but he had risen and washed. He remained in his chamber in his plain breeches, boots and open shirt. The tavern was still quiet, and he knew Rupert stood guard outside the door. He sat with his tea and reviewed his recent correspondence, hoping against hope that he was right about this scheme. He seldom had doubts about his course, but in the final hours before a plan came to its conclusion, it seemed that all the other possibilities became infinitely more plausible.

What if he was wrong about Nathaniel Cushing being the thief?

No, he could not be.

What if he could not prove that Nathaniel Cushing was the thief?

There was a distinct possibility. If Cushing did not take the bait, if he did not try to steal the Eye of India, if he was not caught with it in his possession...Alexander rose to pace his humble chamber, restless with uncertainty.

What if Cushing changed the pattern of his behavior? It would have been ideal to have been at Castle Keyvnor the night before, but Alexander dared not take a second chance when the house was full of guests.

There would be severe repercussions if the true Eye of India was lost in the attempt. Alexander checked upon it again. He had retrieved it from the castle that first night and only Daphne Goodenham knew he had been there. It remained safely in his belongings at the tavern.

And what of Miss Goodenham? How had she guessed that he wore a disguise? Who had she told?

He should have demanded her secrecy instead of assuming it. She might tell her sister, and who could tell where that girl would place her confidence?

Alexander gave a low growl of frustration and wished he had something stronger than tea. It was all too easy to think of his other source of frustration, that tantalizing kiss in the night, and the sweetness of Miss Goodenham's lips. He disliked that Cushing talked to her so much. Surely she could not be Cushing's ally? Surely she could not reveal Alexander?

How could he be certain?

When would he see her again?

How would he know she was trustworthy?

There was a commotion in the tavern below and Alexander frowned at the door. A woman raised her voice, her Scottish brogue thick and her voice high. "I must see His Grace!" she cried, which was remarkable given the early hour.

"His Grace is not receiving guests," Rupert said firmly.

There was the sound of a scuffle and feet racing up the wooden stairs. Rupert swore and heavier footfalls echoed after the lighter ones. Alexander spun to seize his cloak but he was too late. He only had his hand upon it when the door to his chamber was thrown open and a woman in a hooded cloak flung herself toward him.

"Your Grace!" Rupert exclaimed, his annoyance more than clear. "I do apologize. She is as slippery as a fish!"

"Your Grace," the maid cried as she fell prostate at his feet. "I beg you to aid my mistress!"

Alexander was astonished. He might have asked a question, but the maid stretched out her hand, offering a very familiar blue velvet bag.

It was not empty. He could see the shape of the gem through the cloth.

Why had she brought the counterfeit Eye of India to him?

He gestured to the door with an imperious fingertip, knowing it was too late to don his disguise. He would have to hope that the girl did not dare to look into his face. "Remain with us, Haskell, and stand witness to this business."

"Of course, Your Grace." The door was secured and Rupert leaned back against it, his expression one of complete distrust. The maid remained on the floor before Alexander and he could see that she was out of breath.

"Who is your mistress?" he demanded.

"I dare not utter her name, Your Grace," she said and something in her voice was achingly familiar. Alexander took a step closer as the maid lifted her head, letting him see her face for the first time.

It was Miss Goodenham herself.

Who showed considerable promise in mimicry.

"Oh!" she whispered, her eyes lighting and a smile curving her lips as she looked upon him.

"Oh," he replied, then arched a brow. He was both vexed and intrigued, and uncertain which reaction to show her. He indicated the velvet sack. "Where did you get it?"

She lowered her voice to a whisper. "Someone was in my room last night. Eurydice was asleep. I thought it might have been you, sir," she confessed, blushing prettily.

Rupert cleared his throat.

She lifted the bag with a shaking hand. "But I found this in my trunk this morning. I don't know what to do, but I knew you would give me good advice."

So, this was how the gems left the house after they were stolen. Cushing selected a guest with an excess of luggage, relied upon the gem not being discovered before that guest's departure, then retrieved it at some later point. Perhaps he chose someone who openly admired the prize, as Miss Goodenham had.

He recalled Anthea mentioning that they'd encountered Nathaniel Cushing at a tavern on the way home to Inverfyre after the accusations were made against her. He had reportedly been sympathetic about the accusations against her and had shared a meal with Anthea and her companion.

Alexander could imagine that the other man had also retrieved the stolen gem from Anthea's luggage.

But there had been a search. How had the gem not been found in the house where Anthea had stayed? He was missing yet a piece of the puzzle.

His decision made, he turned to Daphne. "Put it back."

She paled. "But it will be missed. There must be a search for such a treasure…"

"There should be, and if there is not, I would ask you to encourage there to be one. A word to the butler should see it done."

Her lips parted in astonishment and she rose unsteadily to her feet. She looked very young and uncertain. "But I should be accused when it is found."

"I wonder if it will be found," Alexander said. "For if it were, there would be no point to the theft."

She frowned and looked down at the velvet sack. "I do not understand."

"Tell me who is given the task of searching your chamber," Alexander advised.

Her eyes lit. "You think the thief will volunteer to assist, that he or she will search my chamber but fail to find the gem!" She bit her lip. "But why?"

"So you would take the gem from the castle, unwittingly."

"And the thief would waylay us somewhere and reclaim it."

"I see no other solution. Do you?"

"It is bold and clever." She stroked the velvet and looked so fearful that he wished to ease away every one of her concerns. "But what if you are wrong, Your Grace?" she asked quietly.

"Then I will defend you to my dying breath, Miss Goodenham," he murmured, holding her gaze so that she could see his conviction.

She shook her head. "I thank you for the sentiment, but your word might not matter, not with something of such value as this prize."

Alexander smiled. "But the value is exactly the key." Her lack of comprehension was clear. "The gem you hold is a fake, Miss Goodenham, created solely to trap the villain."

"Oh!" Her pleasure made her cheeks flush and her eyes sparkle. She lowered her voice to an enticing whisper. "I knew, sir, that if you donned a disguise, it would be for a good reason."

"It is."

"It was this same villain who ensured that your sister's name was tainted," she guessed.

"Indeed it was, and I have vowed to avenge her."

"So, justice will prevail," she said with complete satisfaction.

"Only with your assistance."

"I shall do as you instruct, Your Grace."

The heat of his own pleasure must have shown in his expression, for she modestly dropped her gaze and glanced across the room.

She did not leave, however, which was all the encouragement he needed.

"Might I confide in my sister to see your quest accomplished?" she asked.

"Do you trust her?"

"Utterly," she said without hesitation. "Eurydice would never betray me, nor I her."

Because they had been reliant upon each other

when they were orphaned.

"And she is clever," Miss Goodenham admitted. "I think the prospect of success much higher with her aid."

Alexander nodded understanding, moved more by her trust in Miss Eurydice than her confidence in her sister's wits. "Then by all means, confide in her, but not others, I beg of you."

"It shall be as you say, Your Grace." Still she did not meet his gaze and it seemed to him that her breath came quickly. He guessed that she wished for further reassurance but knew not how to ask for it.

The situation was damnably unconventional.

His gaze rose to Rupert, who evidently was fascinated with the ceiling. Should he send the other man away? His desire for Miss Goodenham was acute, but he would not ruin her and leave her with doubts of his intent. He did not know precisely what he might say to feed her confidence in his honor.

Inspiration came from the fact that Daphne was staring at the vine, which now spilled to the very floor and reached for the ceiling.

Alexander knew its tale might be of aid. "The seed was a gift from my sister," he confessed. "And a legacy of Airdfinnan. I dropped it into water but one night ago."

"But that cannot be! It is of such a size."

"It is said to grow and bloom only when the Laird of Airdfinnan courts a bride."

"Am I wrong that you would be that laird, Your

Grace?" she whispered.

"You are not, and before you ask, I do mean to court a bride once this matter is concluded," he admitted. "To be sure, I had no plan of doing as much, but I met a most beguiling girl, in a tavern, no less."

She flushed and began to smile. "Beguiling, sir?"

"And marvelously perceptive, as well," he agreed and smiled. "I like people who look beyond appearances."

Her gaze clung to his. "As do I, Your Grace."

"It would please me greatly if she granted me some small sign of encouragement."

Alexander barely had time to utter the words before Miss Goodenham cast herself at him with pleasure. He caught her in his arms, savoring the sweet press of her against his chest.

She framed his face in her small hands and studied him intently. "'Twas your eyes that gave you away, sir," she murmured. "You must promise not to look at any other girl so intently before your quest is complete or you might be revealed."

"The quest to name the thief or the quest to have your hand in mine?"

"Both!" she said with a smile.

Alexander chuckled and held her closer. "I vow that I will not," he agreed, then bent to taste her lips again.

Daphne could not believe her good fortune.

The duke was not a fop! No, he was the most handsome man she had ever seen. And he had no ungainly paunch. She had pierced his disguise and even better, he had trusted her with the truth and vowed to defend her. She was convinced that she was the most fortunate woman in all of England, and that was before he kissed her.

It was even better than the first time.

She was the most fortunate woman in all the world.

He broke his kiss and looked down at her, his gaze filled with a lazy satisfaction that thrilled her beyond all else. "My true appearance must remain a secret."

"I will never betray you, Your Grace."

"You cannot even confide this in Eurydice."

"I will not. I pledge it to you." She swallowed. "I vow to be the best wife, Your Grace, and to bear you a dozen sons..."

He smiled. "You will call me Alexander, when we are alone, and I think three sons will do nicely."

"As you wish." Daphne licked her lips. "Alexander."

It felt both sinful and right to say his name, much as kissing him felt both wicked and heavenly.

She smiled at him. "You should call me Daphne, then."

"Indeed, I should." His eyes fairly glowed and the intensity of his look made her shiver. With obvious reluctance, he released her. He seized a dark jacket and a cloak, as well as a large hat. "And now I will see you safely back to the castle."

"But..."

He raised his voice and interrupted her protest before it began. "Upon my word, Haskell, must you bring your wenches and conquests into my own chambers? For all I know, she may have *fleas*!"

"I am sorry, Your Grace," his manservant said, also speaking loudly enough to be overheard.

"Take her away and see her home again, and make haste about it." Then Alexander changed the tone of his voice, sounding for all the world like the manservant. "Of course, Your Grace."

Daphne might have stepped into a play herself.

The manservant spoke shrilly then, mimicking Alexander's foppish voice perfectly. "I would have my chocolate upon your return, Haskell! Hurry, man! I will not be kept waiting for the sake of your wench, no matter how comely she might be!"

"Immediately, Your Grace," Alexander said.

The two men exchanged a wink before Alexander opened the door. He pulled up his hood, then Daphne's as well, then hastened her down the stairs and out of the tavern.

They were barely spared a glance by those arriving to work in the kitchen, and she was spirited toward Castle Keyvnor with impressive speed. He took her through the forests and by paths where they would not be observed, tucking her beneath his cloak when he heard a sound and sweeping her into his arms when he found her pace too slow. The journey was thrilling and all too soon, they approached the castle from behind.

"You are so clever," she said with awe. "You could be upon the stage."

He laughed, a lovely rich sound that made Daphne heat to her toes. "I will give up the disguise once this villain is caught, Daphne, and spend my days beguiling you instead."

"I cannot wait, Your Grace," she whispered and he raised a finger, his eyes gleaming. "Alexander," she corrected. "Though you shall have to convince Grandmaman. She said that you would never wed."

"Fear not, my Daphne. I will win her consent," he growled and Daphne's heart skipped a beat before he kissed her again.

The third time was the best kiss yet.

❦

The thief was awake, for the game came rapidly to its conclusion. He seldom slept until his quarry was securely within his grasp and this time, he sensed that something went awry.

What had that small mark been on the back of the gem? It was new, but not a scratch. A maker's mark and not one he recognized.

It troubled him, deeply.

Something was afoot, though the villain could not name what it was.

He was standing at the window of the chamber he had been given—a small room with a view of the working side of the castle, rather than the sea or the village or even the gates—at the moment that two cloaked figures made a dash from the edge of the woods to the back wall.

Their manner was so furtive that he pressed against the glass, watching.

Were they servants? He could not imagine as much. Every servant was hard at work at this hour of the morning. A noble couple returning from an assignation? There was no doubt that he watched a woman and a man. Did their actions have any relevance to his own plan?

The woman glanced up at the castle walls, just before the couple parted. It was Miss Goodenham, in humble garb. The villain recognized her immediately.

The man's face was not revealed but he left Miss Goodenham at the door and strode back by the same route they had arrived. The villain watched until he disappeared into the shadows of the forest, noting his height and breadth, and his manner of walking. He did not recognize the man, but he was clearly not staying at the keep.

Had Miss Goodenham sought him out? The villain could think of no other way she could have returned in the other man's company.

Could he be the Duke of Inverfyre's man? He had kissed Miss Goodenham before they parted. Would she be so fool as to accept the attentions of a valet? It was difficult to believe she would be so unambitious, but she might be one to put much credit in love.

The greater concern was for the prize that the

villain had thought safely hidden in Miss Goodenham's trunk. Had she discovered and removed it, perhaps granting it to her paramour for safekeeping?

The villain did not know.

And what of that mark? What if the gem was a forgery? He could not fathom how it had been replaced in the single night between its delivery and his theft of it, but what if it had been switched?

What if he had stolen a fake?

How much did Miss Goodenham know?

The villain did not like surprises or uncertainty.

He certainly did not intend to be caught.

Which meant that he had to speak to Miss Goodenham alone and learn the truth of whatever she had done.

No matter what the cost.

CHAPTER FIVE

Eurydice awakened to find that Daphne was gone. Jenny was inexplicably huddled in the corner of the room, still sniffling from her cold. She was wrapped in a blanket from Daphne's bed and looked to be miserable.

Eurydice sat up and felt so chilled that she shivered. How she hated to fall ill! "Where is Daphne?" she asked and the maid lifted a finger to her lips.

"She told me to wait here and be utterly silent," Jenny confessed in a whisper.

"But why?"

The maid shrugged, proving once again that she was possessed of less curiosity than Eurydice. Even if Daphne had been stern and mysterious, Eurydice would have been more interested in the truth than Jenny appeared to be. She made to get out of bed and sneezed again.

"My lady, it seems you had better stay in bed today," Jenny said, still keeping her voice low. "I'll fetch you water to wash, for a change of nightrail will be welcome, as soon as Miss Goodenham returns."

"But where has she gone?" Eurydice asked in exasperation. She could hear the house beginning to stir and she was hungry.

Jenny shrugged again, and then Daphne herself came quickly through the door. She was out of breath from running and dressed in Jenny's clothes. Her hair was only braided but her eyes shone with audacity and satisfaction. She was flushed and delighted in a way that Eurydice did not trust.

Surely her sister had not been so foolish as to meet a man?

Daphne quickly shed the clothes she wore and helped Jenny to don them, then sent the maid for hot water. Once the maid was gone, she hurried to her trunk and tucked something into it before facing Eurydice.

"What are you doing?" Eurydice demanded, sensing a scheme and wanting all the details. "Tell me that you did not have an assignation!"

"Shhhh!" Daphne said, practically flying across the chamber to lay her finger across Eurydice's lips. "Do not speak of it, and keep your voice low no matter what you say."

"Where did you go?"

Daphne glanced to the door and leaned close,

her lips practically against Eurydice's ear. Even so, Eurydice had to concentrate to hear her. "There is a thief in the house and the duke is intent upon catching him," she confided. "I heard someone in our room and found the Eye of India in my trunk this morning. I knew the duke would best advise me what to do."

"You went to him?"

Daphne nodded.

"I imagine you had a shock if you saw him before he was dressed. Is he bald, too?"

Daphne shook her head, impatient with such details. "He bade me put it back and said there would be a search called this morning. If not, I'm to encourage one."

Eurydice sat back in horror. "But then you'll be named..."

"No," Daphne said. "He said he'd defend me if so, but he thinks it will not be so. I am to observe who searches our chamber and report to him."

"Why would the thief hide it here?"

"The duke has a notion that he would see proven." Daphne glanced about herself again then whispered even more quietly, "He thinks the thief uses an unwitting guest as his accomplice to remove his prize from the house, then pilfers that person's luggage later."

"What a devious fiend."

"Indeed."

"And he is here, perhaps a guest at the castle." Already Eurydice was reviewing the list of guests and considering which was most likely to be a jewel thief.

"So it appears." Daphne frowned. "I believe the duke's sister's reputation was soiled by this man and his schemes."

"Then he must be caught."

"Agreed."

Eurydice reflected upon the matter. "If I were to organize a search to find such a missing treasure, I would wait until all the gentlemen were in the dining room, as well as whatever ladies were coming down. I would then search the gentlemen's rooms quietly, without their awareness, and search the ladies' rooms after they had made their way downstairs for the activities of the day. It could all be accomplished with great discretion, save the searching of individual persons."

"Do you think the earl will allow that?"

"Not if he wishes to keep the theft and the search secret. It will be up to the butler, Morris, to orchestrate the details. You should dress and go down for breakfast as soon as possible, to learn as much as you can of their scheme."

"And you?"

Eurydice smiled. "I fear I am too sick to leave our chamber." She sneezed with gusto and pretended to sniffle. "Jenny has already told me to remain in bed. I will do as much and feign sleep. Then I will see who searches our chamber and where he or she looks."

"Jenny should remain with you."

"If I were the thief, I would not search the chamber until she was gone."

"Do you think it quite safe for you to be alone here?"

"Perhaps not, but it is devilishly exciting." Eurydice smiled. "Like something from a novel. Return before luncheon and I will tell you what I have seen. After all, I would not have you be without tidings for your duke."

Daphne gripped her hand. "Thank you, Eurydice."

"I still cannot fathom what you find appealing about the man."

Her sister's smile was quick and triumphant. "Perhaps love works in mysterious ways."

"Love?!" Despite her protestation, not another word about the duke could Eurydice pry from Daphne's lips.

❧

Daphne listened with care as she descended the main staircase. She could hear the murmur of men's voices, and thought she detected a thread of urgency. The earl was conferring quietly with the butler, Morris, the pair of them very solemn.

"And are you not a fine sight with which to greet the day, Miss Goodenham?" Mr. Cushing demanded cheerfully, his voice behind Daphne enough to make her jump. "I daresay you are the prettiest girl in Cornwall."

"I thank you, sir," she said, taking his elbow to

continue into the dining room. "Do you mean to ride today?"

"Oh, I think not," he said easily, then wagged a finger at her. "You neglected to give me a tour yesterday."

"Indeed, I did. I am sorry but my grandmother required our attendance."

"And I am heartbroken," he said lightly. "Would you do the honors this morning instead?"

Daphne frowned as Gryffyn Cardew joined the other two men and their murmuring continued.

The theft had been discovered then, and they were deciding what to do.

She continued to chatter, as if oblivious, though her heart was skipping. "I had thought of taking a walk in the garden," Daphne said.

"Oh, but that would suit me perfectly!" Mr. Cushing said. "Is it true that there is a maze?"

"A very fine one, sir."

"Then I would entreat you to show it to me this very morning." He made a pout, although his eyes were twinkling. "Otherwise, Miss Goodenham, my heart may never recover from the blow you have dealt it."

Daphne laughed, as she was certain she was meant to. She truly didn't care about showing Mr. Cushing any detail of the house or garden, but she supposed she should behave as if all were normal. The duke could act brilliantly, so she would try to do the same. The gentlemen in the foyer clearly came to some agreement with Morris. The butler then conferred with Mrs. Bray before the pair set off together.

There was purpose in their strides.

But if only Morris and Mrs. Bray did the searches, did that mean one of them was the thief?

Or had Alexander been mistaken?

Daphne's throat tightened with the prospect of the Eye of India being found in her trunk. What would her grandmother say? What could she do? She had promised the duke to do as instructed, and this was but the first test of her obedience.

She would not fail him.

❦

It was the housekeeper, Mrs. Bray, who knocked on the door.

"Whatever are *you* doing here?" she demanded when Jenny opened the door.

"Lady Eurydice is ill, Mrs. Bray, and thought I should attend to her..."

Eurydice managed to summon an impressive sneeze. She sniffled and dabbed at her eyes as the housekeeper surveyed her with disapproval. "Good morning, Mrs. Bray," she said, ensuring that she sounded as if her nose was blocked.

"If I may say so, it does not appear to be a good day for you, Miss Eurydice," the older woman said sourly, then turned to Jenny again. "What you should do is tell Nelson of your mistress' illness so that Lady North Barrows is fully aware of the situation."

"Yes, Mrs. Bray."

"I suggest you do so immediately."

Jenny cast a glance at Eurydice.

"It would be very sensible, Jenny," Eurydice said. "Please go."

No sooner had the door closed behind the maid, then Mrs. Bray fixed Eurydice with a look. "I do apologize for the inconvenience, miss, but there has been a theft. Morris has instructed me to search the baggage of lady guests in the remote chance that the Eye of India has been...misplaced."

Eurydice strove to appear both surprised and alarmed. "The Eye of India? Isn't that the gem that was given to Lady Tamsyn?"

"The very same."

"I cannot imagine how it might be in our luggage."

The housekeeper gave her a quelling look. "Surely you do not wish to obstruct the course of justice, Miss Eurydice?"

"Surely not, Mrs. Bray," Eurydice said, clenching her hands together beneath the sheets. Was Mrs. Bray the thief? It did seem unlikely.

But if the housekeeper wasn't the thief, then the duke had given Daphne bad advice. The gem would be found and Daphne would be accused of taking it. Had her sister granted her trust in the wrong place?

Eurydice could scarcely breathe in her terror, but she did her best to continue the ruse of being ill. To be sure, she did not have to do it long.

Within moments, Mrs. Bray had found the gem.

She froze in the act of searching Daphne's trunk, then straightened slowly with the velvet sack in her hand. She opened it and Eurydice saw a flash of the stones, then Mrs. Bray turned to face her with it on her palm. "I suppose you know nothing of how this came to be here?"

Eurydice didn't have to pretend to be shocked. "Nothing!" she squeaked. "Daphne would never have taken it. She doesn't even take my hair ribbons!"

The grim housekeeper did not reply. She simply left the room, inclining her head briefly to Eurydice, then called for Morris.

Eurydice felt truly ill then.

Daphne was doomed.

She flung herself from the bed and began to dress with haste.

❧

Alexander paced in his chamber at the tavern. He had to leave time for the trap to be sprung, but he did not like that Daphne was alone and undefended. He was tense. Uncertain. Fearful of the outcome.

"You are going to the castle for luncheon," Rupert murmured, his tone reassuring. He was polishing Alexander's boots. "She cannot find much trouble in the span of several hours."

"I would argue that a girl could find boundless trouble in so much time as that," Alexander replied grimly. "I, for example, could have ruined her in

113

thirty minutes."

"Given your recent chastity and her beauty, it might have only taken ten."

Alexander glared at his friend, not so much because he was annoyed but because he felt it was expected.

Rupert grinned. He then sobered. "Are you certain you should have trusted her?"

"Why would I not have done so?"

"She could be part of the scheme. The villain might mean to draw you out. You did, after all, walk with her after church yesterday."

"And so?"

"And so, if the thief guesses your role, he might have chosen her as an ally in exposing you. She might be in his trust and sent to draw you out."

Alexander shook his head, trusting his instinctive sense of her honesty. "Daphne has no guile."

"She might be a pawn, used without her awareness that she is being so manipulated."

There was a prospect that Alexander could not readily refute.

Before he could summon a reply, there was a sound from the table before the fire. He spun to see that the vine had dropped a large bud, which had made a noise when striking the floor. He might have expected that the blooms would eventually fade, but another fell with a thud as he was watching. In fact, there were no open flowers left at all. They were all either closed or closing, their hue turning as dark as midnight, and more of them fell before his eyes.

The vine even seemed to wilt, drooping with no hint of its former vigor.

"Finally, that wretched thing reaches its limit. I had wondered what we were to do with it on our departure," Rupert began but Alexander held up a hand.

"It thrives when the laird's courtship finds favor," he said with resolve. "That is the tale. Either she has turned against me, or she is in peril." His voice rose to a roar. "My boots! My jacket! A horse, for the love of God!"

"Aye, go," Rupert replied, taking the foppish tone of Alexander's disguise. "Leave me with this mess of a cravat while you pursue your paramour!"

Alexander realized that his friend was thinking more clearly than he was. It would be much quicker for him to leave if he pretended to be Haskell.

That man continued as he gave Alexander the dark jacket and cloak, helping him dress with all haste. "I tell you, Haskell, one more *billet-doux* and we are finished. Finished! If I cannot rely upon your undivided attention, then I have no need of your services at all!" He dropped his voice. "Take the bay. She is more than ready to run."

Alexander nodded and left the chamber as Haskell complained mightily about his supposed shortcomings, hoping with every step that he reached Daphne in time.

Daphne did not manage to eat much more than

a morsel at breakfast, although the food was delicious. She smiled and nodded, but had little idea what was said to her.

Morris came into the dining room, his expression stern, and bent to whisper something to Mr. Cushing. That man excused himself and left the room, and Daphne swallowed in her fear.

She excused herself and left the dining room, heading back to the chamber she shared with Eurydice. She wanted desperately to know what had happened in her absence.

She only made it to the base of the stairs before Mr. Cushing came striding out of the library. He seized her elbow and fairly shoved her into a parlor. "Quickly!" he said in a whisper. "We must hurry!"

His manner was so imperious that Daphne obeyed. It was only when he closed and locked the door behind them that she wondered at his scheme. "But why? What is amiss?"

Someone called her name from the corridor. Daphne thought it was the earl, but Mr. Cushing shoved her toward the doors that opened to the gardens. "They mean to hunt the duke and his man," he whispered. "It is a terrible mistake. We have to warn him!"

Alarm surged through Daphne. "Of course! I will just fetch my cloak."

Mr. Cushing's grip tightened on her arm. "There is no time! You can wear my jacket," he said, shedding it and wrapping it around her. "Quickly!"

Daphne did as instructed, terrified for

Alexander. "What did you hear? What is this about?"

"The Eye of India," Mr. Cushing said, urging her across the lawn. "It was stolen."

"No!" Daphne protested because she thought she should.

She had expected they would either go to the stables to fetch horses or walk toward the village. Mr. Cushing, though, was leading her toward the maze.

What was he doing?

"Yes," he said with conviction and she noticed a hardness in his eyes that she had not seen before. "And worse, the one they recovered is a forgery." He flung her forward, casting her into the maze so savagely that she stumbled. She realized belatedly that no one would be able to see them.

He seized his coat, hauling it from her shoulders and leaving her shivering as he glared down at her. "Where is it, Miss Goodenham?"

"Where is what?" she asked, retreating carefully.

"The real Eye of India," Mr. Cushing said, taking measured steps in pursuit. She could not believe she had ever thought him charming and good-natured. "What have you done with it?"

"Nothing!" Daphne backed away, rounding a corner. Could she get a confession from him for Alexander? Could she be of assistance to her duke in disguise?

"But you met someone this morning."

"How do you know that?" With every question,

Daphne retreated further into the maze. She had no choice. She could not pass Mr. Cushing and she didn't want him to touch her.

"I saw from the window," he said with a sneer. "And that kiss, as well. Who was it? Did you give it to him?"

"I gave nothing to anyone," she declared, which was true. He raised a hand, but she spoke first. "Were you the one who put the gem in my trunk?"

Mr. Cushing laughed. "So you did find it."

"It was there when I went to breakfast. Did you put it there?"

"Of course, I did. Who else has the wits to steal such gems with perfect success?"

"It is not so perfect a success if there is only a forgery remaining," she could not help but say.

He struck her then, slapping her across the face. His blow stung and revealed his true nature. "Where is the real gem now?"

"I don't know. Perhaps you took it back."

"Liar!" He lunged after her with fury in his eyes and Daphne fled. "I will have the gem!" he snarled and she ran as quickly as she could.

She knew she was going deeper into the maze. She knew she hadn't paid nearly enough attention to find her way back out. But with such a villain in hot pursuit, she feared she had little chance of escape.

"Alexander!" she screamed with all her might, hoping against hope that her duke was close enough to hear her.

Alexander galloped the bay toward Castle Keyvnor. He heard Daphne scream his name and the sound was enough to make his blood run cold.

Sadly, he could not tell where she was. The gardens were enormous and seemingly empty. She could be on the parapet walk or at a window. He pulled the horse up short and turned it in place, uncertain where to look.

"You there!" a girl cried and he spied a young woman racing toward him.

It was Miss Eurydice.

"Please, sir, you must help my sister!" she said. "He dragged her into the maze..."

She managed to say no more before Alexander gave the mare his heels. He leaped from the saddle at the entrance to the maze and strode inside. He paused to listen and heard a woman catch her breath.

"You lying vermin," she said. "*You* stole the Eye of India."

"I never suggested otherwise."

"But you lied to the earl and to your uncle," Daphne said. "They both trusted you, Mr. Cushing, but you deceived them."

"Great Uncle Timothy thought I was stupid," Cushing said, a sneer in his tone. "He liked keeping me poor, passing expensive gems through my hands, rubbing my nose in the fact that I'd never be able to afford even the smallest stone in his collection. He could have given the Eye of India to me! I would have sold it for a fortune! It would have changed my life. But no, he had to give it to some niece who barely remembered that he existed."

On stealthy feet, Alexander proceeded further into the maze. Could it be that Daphne knew he was there? Was she aiding him to get a confession of guilt? If so, she was a marvel worth every luxury he could shower upon her.

"But this can't be the first gem you've stolen?" she taunted. "You can't call yourself a brilliant thief if you've stolen only once and then been left with a forgery."

Cushing swore and Alexander moved more quickly in pursuit.

"Of course it's not the first. I'm notorious."

"But still you're said to be penniless." Daphne sighed. "I think perhaps you're not so clever after all."

"I lose at cards because they cheat me!" Cushing roared. Alexander heard Daphne make a little gasp and then her running footfalls. Cushing crashed after her, Alexander following. Deeper into the maze they went until there was suddenly the sound of a fall.

Followed by silence. Alexander eased around a shrub to find Cushing creeping toward a corner ahead. The toe of a familiar slipper could be seen beyond the turn of the maze.

The crash had been the sound of her falling.

She must be unconscious.

She must be injured.

Cushing leaped around the corner, and

Alexander saw the astonishment on his face just before he saw Daphne's small fist. She tried to strike him, but Cushing recovered quickly enough to seize her wrist.

He didn't manage to twist it behind her back, because Alexander grabbed Cushing by the collar, spun him around and punched him in the nose. He struck the other man in the gut, then in the chin, so that he fell moaning to the ground.

Daphne smiled at Alexander with pleasure. "I knew you would come," she said, then her lips worked. "Did you hear his confession, Haskell?"

Alexander smiled that she understood the ruse instinctively. "All of it, my lady. You have ensured his condemnation."

Daphne had also proven that she was utterly trustworthy and that his instincts about her had been right.

"Good," she said, surveying the fallen man with disapproval. "I despise dishonesty in a man."

Alexander heard Eurydice arrive behind him, her breath coming quickly, and doubtless some measure of the household following behind, given the noise.

"Miss Goodenham," he said, bowing to her even as he seethed that there was a bruise rising on her cheek. "His Grace, the Duke of Inverfyre, sent me to enquire as to whether you and your grandmother, Lady North Barrows, might accept a call from him this afternoon."

Daphne's smile was radiant. "I should be delighted, Haskell. I am certain that my grandmother will also be amenable. Please do take my every encouragement to His Grace."

"I will and I am glad that the timing of my arrival was so fortuitous."

"As am I, Haskell. You have my thanks."

Alexander glanced at the earl. "But first, I will see this ruffian taken into the custody of the magistrate." He pulled a velvet sack from his pocket, for this was his chance to put the real gem in the earl's possession. "And this prize returned to where it rightfully belongs."

"An excellent plan, Haskell," Daphne said and it took everything within Alexander to keep from bestowing a triumphant kiss upon her lips.

That would have to wait until the afternoon, assuming that Lady North Barrows accepted his offer for Daphne's hand.

"I find it most curious," Eurydice said that night when the sisters were alone in their chamber together dressing for dinner.

"That the duke should want to marry me?" Daphne teased, certain that nothing could be better in her world. All had been explained to the earl and the true gem exchanged for the replica, Nathaniel Cushing had been taken into custody and through it all, Alexander had pretended to be his own man, Haskell.

He had arrived in his full splendor in the afternoon to ask for Daphne's hand in marriage.

Grandmaman had been surprised and had only agreed when Daphne entreated her to do as much. The match was a brilliant one for Daphne, to be sure. If *Grandmaman* cast a more shrewd glance over Alexander after that, it could not be that much of a surprise.

Alexander had brought a salve for Daphne and insisted upon applying it to her cheek with his own fingers, the blue simmer of his gaze making her feel adored indeed.

Matters could not be better.

She sighed contentment and scarce even listened to Eurydice. Her sister had been over Nathaniel's scheme repeatedly, apparently fascinated with the doings of crime.

"Not that," Eurydice said with impatience. "I meant Haskell's eyes."

"His eyes?"

"They were blue today when he rode to your rescue. Indeed, they were like blue fire."

"Yes," Daphne agreed happily.

"But I am quite certain that at the tavern, they were brown."

Daphne blinked. "You might have been mistaken," she dared to say. "We barely glimpsed him at the tavern."

"I do not think so," Eurydice said with her usual conviction. "I noticed that they were quite nice eyes. I wouldn't forget them."

Daphne exhaled. "What a shame it is that you couldn't look again today, what with him riding immediately for the magistrate."

"It is a shame," her sister agreed. "I shall have to take a closer look once we arrive in London. Are we truly going to stay in the duke's house in Grosvenor Square?"

"Yes!" Daphne said, accepting the change of subject with relief. "He said it made more sense, since *Grandmaman* would have to let a house and his is simply sitting there, awaiting the pleasure of her arrival."

"She liked that turn of phrase," Eurydice said, which was true. "And we are casting him out?"

"Not exactly. She said he should stay somewhere else until we are married." Daphne realized that his impassioned response might have been what changed her grandmother's mind about the match. "He said he would get a special license instead."

"He does want to marry you!"

"And I cannot wait to marry him," Daphne said. All she wanted truly was an hour alone with Alexander, but she had a feeling that what they might do in that hour was better accomplished after their marriage vows had been exchanged.

She thought of the thrum in his voice when he had vowed to get that license and knew their match would be one of the happiest of all time.

She would ensure it was so.

In his room at the Mermaid's Kiss, Alexander savored a sip of brandy and considered the success of the day. He glanced out the window at the lights of Castle Keyvnor and felt unusual impatience to reach London. He had to push aside the vine to make space on the table to write his letter. It had recovered from its state earlier in the day and was on the cusp of blooming again.

The wretched story was true, after all.

He hoped the plant would fit in his coach, though he might have to ride with the driver for that to be so.

There was no question of leaving it behind or letting it perish. Daphne adored it and he was rather fond of its role in ensuring her safety on this day.

He picked up his quill, summoned the familiar tone, and began to write.

My dear Aunt Penelope—

Such news I have to share with you on this merry Christmastide! You will be heartened to learn that Dr. MacEwan's prescription worked admirably—I am fully restored to my former vigor, but it is not due to the sea air. I arrived in Cornwall to witness such excitement that it has driven all illness from me. Haskell chose the destination of Bocka Morrow when I told him to find accommodation in Cornwall, and for a reason of his own. It has been revealed that Haskell is a spy—yes, Haskell!—and he succeeded in unveiling a notorious jewel thief at Castle Keyvnor. The fiend stole a gift from one of the brides, but Haskell saw him apprehended. Even now, he journeys to London with the magistrate to see the villain brought to justice.

Of course, this put me in mind of Anthea's perfectly dreadful experience. You will be delighted to know that this same man was responsible for that offense, so justice has been served. He used the most enchanting young lady here to aid in his scheme. Once all was revealed, I could only express my heartfelt sympathy to her for enduring even a short-lived shadow upon her good name. In the end, she proved to be such a delight that she and I are to wed. You might know her grandmother, the dowager Viscountess North Barrows? I remember my grandfather talking of the Lord North Barrows' nuptials to that very lady...

And we shall soon have the pleasure of each other's company! I have sent word with Haskell to open the house in Grosvenor Square and will escort my betrothed, Miss Goodenham there, along with her sister, Eurydice, and Lady North Barrows herself. I had thought to leave the house to the ladies until Daphne and I celebrate our nuptials, but with each passing day, I see greater appeal in a special license. I will invite you to dinner to meet my intended once we have arrived in Town. I do indeed hope that Anthea can be coaxed to join us shortly. Daphne has a great deal of shopping to be done before the season and we both know what excellent taste Anthea has...

EPILOGUE

Anthea Armstrong was not surprised to receive a letter from her brother shortly after Christmas. She had been hoping to hear from him since his departure, and while Christmas had been festive, it had also been lonely. She missed Alexander's laughter.

It was snowing lightly and she sat before the fire in the library to read his missive, daring to hope it held tidings of his return. It was a nice fat letter, and she looked forward to a goodly amount of news.

To her surprise, Alexander's letter was folded around a plumper missive. His message was surprisingly short.

My dear Anthea—

The seed sprouted.

You lost the wager.

I look forward to seeing you at the London house so that you can meet my betrothed, Miss Daphne Goodenham.

I shall let Daphne recount the tale of our whirlwind courtship, in all the fulsome detail that ladies so adore.

Suffice it to say that I am well content and hope that you will ensure that Daphne's first season is a triumphant one. I mean to stay in London long enough for Daphne to tire of its charms, then retreat to Airdfinnan. Please join us with all speed.

With greatest affection,
Your brother—
Alexander

It was marked with his seal.

Anthea was pleased by the news, though a little troubled by the notion of going to London.

Although she had made Alexander a wager.

She had to stand by her own terms.

She wondered, too, that Alexander had found a bride so quickly and feared the lady in question might not love him sufficiently well. The last thing he needed was a repeat of Miranda Delaney's betrayal.

Anthea opened the other letter with curiosity. Daphne's writing was graceful, the letters elegant and regular but not overly ornate. Even without reading a word, Anthea was half-convinced that Alexander had found an honest and beautiful girl to make his bride.

Dear Lady Anthea—

I am writing to introduce myself to you at Alexander's suggestion, though I would much prefer to do so in person. He seems to think that you will be skeptical of my existence without a letter from me, though why you might doubt his word is a complete mystery. He is the most honorable and constant man I have ever known, and already I trust in his word implicitly.

He told me that the seed of the vine was a gift from you, and I must thank you for giving it to him. Not only did it grow into the most beautiful plant, but its vigor seemed to encourage Alexander to trust in me. I have a curious sense that our courtship might not have come to so happy or so quick a resolution without those red flowers in his buttonhole. They truly are splendid and their scent is enchanting beyond all else. Even now, Alexander seeks a way to take the vine with us to London that it might be planted at the house in Grosvenor Square. I greatly look forward to seeing the original vine, with its fearsome thorns, on the walls of Airdfinnan.

Perhaps you will tell me the tale of Bayard of Villonne who first brought the vine to Airdfinnan. Alexander's version of the story seems to be short and lacking in romantic detail. I do hope that you will come to London for our nuptials, and also to offer me your advice. Alexander means to stay for the season, which is very exciting, but it will be my first and I would not wish to make a misstep. I should welcome your assistance.

I confess that I have always yearned to have an older sister, instead of always being the older sister, and so your existence is yet another wish of mine come true thanks to Alexander. I hope that we will also be friends, but truly, if you have any traits in common with Alexander, I know that I will love you dearly. There will be those, I am sure, who think our match a hasty one, but the truth is simple and I share it willingly—the Duke of Inverfyre, were he known by any other name, would be just as beloved by me as he is in this moment. I would adore Alexander if he were penniless. I never thought to meet such a man, and I am awed that I shall be his bride

.

If you doubt the truth, you are welcome to ask my sister, Eurydice, who is always glad to surrender my deepest secrets to others. She has not a shred of artifice and is terribly clever—Alexander has told her of his library and she has already ensured her invitation to Airdfinnan. She may well set foot in his library and never be seen again.

I eagerly await the opportunity to meet you, my new sister. With affection—
Miss Daphne Goodenham

Anthea read the letter twice. It was impossible to overlook the delight in Daphne's letter or to fail to note both her affection for her sister and her adoration of Alexander. Even Alexander's short message held a distinct note of satisfaction, and Anthea could well imagine his contented smile.

She wanted to *see* his smile and meet both Daphne and Eurydice.

Anthea took a fortifying breath and made her decision. She rang for Findlay before she could change her mind and watched the falling snow with her heart hammering as she waited for him. She felt a curious mix of satisfaction, trepidation and excitement, one that she had always associated with journeys to London.

"Yes, my lady?" Findlay said and she turned to him with a smile.

"Good news, Findlay. My brother is betrothed and will marry in London in the new year."

"Fine news indeed, my lady."

"And I will journey there to join them."

If Findlay was surprised that she meant to leave Airdfinnan, he hid it well. "Very good, my lady."

"I shall stay through the season. My brother wishes his bride to have her fair measure of London society and I hope I can enhance her enjoyment."

"Of course, my lady."

"I would like to leave in the morning, Findlay, and would appreciate you accompanying me to take charge of the London house. I believe there will be parties, as Alexander seems in a celebratory mood. Could you send Connaught to help me pack?"

"Of course, my lady." Findlay bowed, then hesitated before departing.

"Yes, Findlay? Is there something else?"

"Only that it is good to see you with a sparkle in your eye again, my lady," the older man said. He had been in the service of the family for so long that Anthea did not think his comment impertinent. "I do not doubt that this foray to London will be far merrier than your last."

Anthea's heart warmed. "Thank you, Findlay," she said, her voice a little husky. He gave her a nod and a glance that was encouraging, if not paternal, then departed to do her bidding. Anthea opened Daphne's letter and read it again, feeling her anticipation rise.

Two more sisters.

She dared to hope that Airdfinnan's butler was right.

A BARON FOR ALL SEASONS
The Brides of North Barrows #3

Rupert Haskell has always thought that Anthea, his friend Alexander's younger sister, would make an excellent choice of bride, but the loss of his inheritance made it impossible for him to court her. Caught between his honor and his heart, the only way he can show his esteem for Anthea is remove the stain from her name—even if that means having to watch her marry another man.

Anthea Armstrong left London in her debut season when she was falsely accused of theft. Now that the real villain has been apprehended, she's returned to town to arrange her brother's wedding. She hopes to once again encounter the mysterious suitor who stole her heart with a kiss at a masquerade ball...when she realizes the mysterious man is none other than Rupert Haskell, can she convince this proud man of honor to take a chance on love?

Available Now!

Download a free family tree for the *Brides of North Barrows* at Claire's website:

https://delacroix.net/north-barrows/

ABOUT THE AUTHOR

Deborah Cooke sold her first book in 1992, a medieval romance called **Romance of the Rose** published under her pseudonym Claire Delacroix. Since then, she has published over fifty novels in a wide variety of sub-genres, including historical romance, contemporary romance, and paranormal romance. She has published under the names Claire Delacroix, Claire Cross and Deborah Cooke. **The Beauty**, part of her successful Bride Quest series of historical romances, was her first title to land on the *New York Times* List of Bestselling Books. Her books routinely appear on other bestseller lists and have won numerous awards. In 2009, she was the writer-in-residence at the Toronto Public Library, the first time the library has hosted a residency focused on the romance genre. In 2012, she was honored to receive the Romance Writers of America's Mentor of the Year Award.

Currently, she writes historical romances as Claire Delacroix. She also writes paranormal romances and contemporary romances under the name Deborah Cooke. Deborah lives in Canada with her husband and family, as well as far too many unfinished knitting projects.

To learn more about her books, visit her websites:
http://delacroix.net
http://deborahcooke.com

A Duke By Any Other Name

Made in the USA
Monee, IL
16 January 2024

51915946R00081